These Eyes
So Green

Deborah Kelsey

ISBN 978-1-936556-76-2

Published 2016
Published by Black Velvet Seductions Publishing

Published 2016
Printed by Black Velvet Seductions Publishing
A division of Savage Publications

Visit us at:
www.blackvelvetseductions.com

For Uwe

Chapter One

Standartenführer Hans Faber knocked on the door of his superior officer's office and waited for the entreaty to enter, then opened the door and went in. He stopped to give the salute and a hearty "Heil Hitler!" before coming to stand before Gruppenführer Peter Kuhl's desk, which loomed large in the small office, covered as it was with the accoutrements of a Major General of the Third Reich, including a sterling silver pen and inkwell.

"This one, Hans, is different." Gruppenführer Kuhl tossed a file across the desk to Faber, who took it and opened it to examine the two photos.

Kuhl knew that if anyone could handle this case, it would be Faber. He watched Faber closely as he perused the file. He had always admired this dapper figure. Faber stood elegant and immaculate in his uniform before his Gruppenführer, who had always felt rather clumsy by comparison in his officer's attire.

Kuhl had always regretted the fact that he had never mastered the art of having a uniform properly tailored, and he resented Faber's skill in this area. He had once happened to be at the tailor's when Faber was being measured for his uniform. Kuhl watched him as he turned slowly and viewed himself in his uniform from every possible angle, instructing the tailor in each proper placement of pin and tuck. Faber seemed to consider tailoring as a finely choreographed dance of movement and observation. From what the tailor had told him, Kuhl knew it took Faber a good hour to complete the process, and the results were always stunning. At 170cm, Faber was not a tall man by any means, yet he seemed much taller; more confident and more in command in his uniform; which annoyed Kuhl, who towered over him, in addition to outranking him.

Faber finished flipping through the file and returned to the two photos of the suspect in question. One of them was of a rather grubby-looking farm boy in a broad cap, the other of a raven-haired woman of such fierce beauty he nearly caught his breath. There was something oddly familiar in her dark, intelligent eyes, and to think that the disheveled farm boy and this striking woman were one and the same brought a faint smile to his lips.

"Clever," he said, "very clever. She is quite stunning, but rather conspicuously so, hence the alter ego, I imagine." He tossed the open file back onto the desk. "She's not Jewish? She looks Jewish."

"No, "answered Kuhl. "She was born in the Sudetenland. Her parents died in the flu epidemic, but they left her some money. She was a student at the Sorbonne, and then worked as a photographer in Paris; led the Bohemian lifestyle; and a rather wild one, by all accounts. She did not marry, but had a child; a son. She wanted to raise him in the country and ended up in Angouleme. For many years now she has had a small business running vegetables and fruits to the groceries and cafes in the area. But more than a few believe that she runs other things as well; weapons to the resistance, to be exact. Not much is known about Desiree Mendelsohn except that she once used her alter ego very effectively," Kuhl went on. "'He' saved her life on more than one occasion. But that's not what differentiates her from other members of the Resistance. There's a touch of wildness in her; a passion that sets her apart from others we've pursued in the Resistance."

Faber glanced back down at the photo, intrigued. "A passion," he murmured. He could see it in those dark yet fiery eyes.

"Yes. This woman makes love as fiercely as she has been known to fight; with women as well as men, but she clearly prefers men."

"And how do we know this?" asked Faber, his interest piqued.

"Because, although Desiree Mendelsohn will make love enthusiastically to a woman, throughout her life she has fallen in love only with men." Kuhl was firm in this declaration.

"Aha. Men are her weakness, then." Faber smiled.

"Oh yes. And that very weakness will be her undoing," Kuhl smiled, his voice calculating.

"And how is that?" Faber was bewildered.

"That will be entirely up to you," Kuhl pronounced, looking him straight in the eye.

Faber burst out laughing, and Kuhl felt his cheeks blush. Although he outranked Faber, he had never lost a sense of acute inferiority in the man's presence. Faber never failed to exude confidence and self-assurance, especially in areas of sexual matters; whereas Kuhl, for all his honors and achievements on the battlefield, in matters of a sexual nature still felt like the boy who had always been bested on the football field.

After a few last chuckles, Faber quickly caught his breath. "Forgive me, Herr Gruppenführer," he said, amusement still clear in his voice, "but you can't mean that I am to serve as your male Mata Hari?"

"In a sense, yes. Oh, come now, Hans. You've always been a ladies' man. You've been through half the actresses from UFA film studios. Your conquests are legendary."

"Simply rumors, Sir. I enjoy women, yes; I sleep with as many of them as I can, but I am not what the Americans would crudely call a 'stud horse'."

"You've said that rumors often expose the truth." Kuhl felt triumphant, knowing he had made the right choice with Faber.

"Hoist by my own petard," Faber grinned. "Well, from the looks of it—or, I should say, of her—this should prove to be a very pleasant assignment."

"You have a way with women, Hans. Everyone knows it." There was more than a touch of envy in Kuhl's voice.

"I had no idea that my 'exploits' had become the stuff of legend," Faber replied with a broad grin.

Kuhl suddenly grew more serious. "Let me make myself very clear, Standartenführer. This is not a woman who is easily intimidated. If anything, violence only makes her more determined. What she does respond to is seduction, and we both know that's your forte."

Faber picked up the file once more, and removed the photo of the womanly Desiree. Again he found himself struck by those deep brown eyes, and the curious sensation that she was somehow familiar to him.

"If she is as fiercely passionate in bed as you say, she and I should make quite a match," Faber mused, gazing again at those beautiful dark eyes. What would she be like in bed, he wondered. He was sure he would soon find out…

Gruppenführer Kuhl interrupted his thoughts. "And that's precisely why you are the man to not only captivate, and thus capture her, but to tame her as well. Take her to your bed, Hans, then bring her back to us—refreshed and ready to talk."

***

Faber studied the file thoroughly as his staff car drove him back to his fashionable flat. He discovered that, in less than two years, Desiree Mendelsohn had made quite a name for herself. She had initially fought the occupation. Her son, then fifteen, had been killed during the fight in their small town outside Paris. Some accounts in the files said that Desiree had been forever changed by the loss of her son. She had become a hedonist as well as a fighter. In reading the accounts Faber thought that she seemed not unlike Hans himself; determined and self-assured. Reading further, he found that it had never been proven that Desiree had any association with the Resistance. All that was known was that she would disappear for a week or two at a time in her small panel truck, but she always returned with a load of fruit and vegetables for her customers. Most intriguing to Hans was the fact that, a year ago, Desiree had been charged with smuggling foodstuffs and sent to a concentration camp. In that camp she had had a lover; an SS officer who had managed to have her released, only to find himself sent to the Eastern front a month later, where he had been killed. It was rumored that this love affair with an SS officer had brought Desiree back to life again after the devastating loss of her son, and it was believed by many that this was the reason why she now maintained a neutral and occasionally friendly relationship with the occupying forces. Hans closed the file again. Who knows what drives a woman to think and feel and act the way she does, he pondered, as he gazed once more at Desiree's photo. He had always felt that a woman was a labyrinth of secrets to be explored and uncovered, and, as he suspected in Desiree's case, she would need to be thoroughly unleashed to revel in her charms. In the short time he had known about her, Desiree had already crept into his psyche, had stirred both his intellect and his sensuality; something very few women had done. Hans knew that this case would challenge him as both an inquisitive SS officer and a gifted detective. He also realized that it would prove stimulating to both his body and his mind.

***

Rene Charlont waved to Desiree Mendelsohn as her truck pulled up before his restaurant, Lune, and greeted her with a hearty hello. He watched her womanly figure as she hopped out of the truck. He had always had a crush on her, and he knew she knew it.

Desiree hefted several baskets of tomatoes from her truck and handed them to Rene's fresh-faced assistant.

"And that's it," she said to Rene, "enough tomatoes to last you for more than a week. I've labeled each basket according to the degree of ripeness and how long the fruit should be kept refrigerated before being brought to room temperature to continue the ripening process."

Desiree smiled at Rene. Both of them were well into their forties, she thought, and they had each reached that point in their lives when they were at last comfortable in their own skins, and so much more at ease in the world. They had been friends now for over ten years.

The cheerful, plump-cheeked restaurateur grinned broadly at the lush and handsome woman. Even with the occupation, Charlont could easily claim to be content and at peace with himself, but he knew that wasn't quite the case with Desiree. There was a restlessness in her; a yearning that kept her more youthful, as though she were still searching for something. That very restlessness, Charlont knew, had also taken her in and out of more than a few beds.

"You never cease to amaze me, Desiree," Charlont laughed. "How can one woman locate so many fresh vegetables"

"Once again, my dear Rene, the tomato is not a vegetable. It is a fruit. It has seeds." Although her voice was serious, Desiree's deep brown eyes twinkled as she spoke.

"So does a pepper," Charlont remarked, his grin still broad as he plucked a shiny green one from one of the newly delivered baskets.

"And it, too, is a fruit." Desiree looked straight into his good-humored eyes and winked.

Charlont laughed again. "How is it, Cherie, that in all the years we've known each other, I have never been your lover? Why have I not been blessed with the opportunity?"

"You've always had the opportunity," Desiree replied. "You're just too much of a gentleman to take advantage of it."

The two friends enjoyed a good chuckle together; then Charlont suddenly grew serious. He stepped forward and put one of his large, beefy hands onto Desiree's shoulder, rubbing it affectionately.

"Never forget," he said, "that if you should need me for anything— anything at all—I will be there for you."

"And that, mon ami, is why we have never been lovers," Desiree replied as she turned away to climb back into her panel truck. She started the engine and, with a last wave, pulled away from Rene's storefront.

Yes, Renee, Desiree thought as she drove away, I can count on you.

That's why you are not my lover. She thought back to a time that felt like a hundred years ago. But what about Uwe? He had been her lover, and he saved her life. The thought, always unbidden, had a habit of popping back into Desiree's head. She thought about Uwe, and the strange mix of tenderness and brutality that had been their relationship. The kindnesses he showed her in the extra food and the comforts he smuggled to her, the easy work details he had always managed to arrange. Yet at the same time he was violently, furiously passionate with her in bed. He was feral and completely uninhibited, as though the physical act of love was the one part of his life in which he could completely let go and wrestle with everything that angered and frightened and excited him all at once.

Desiree had surprised herself by meeting his passion and thoroughly unleashing her own. In Uwe's bed she had uncovered parts of herself she hadn't known existed; raw, dark places, and a physical and emotional hunger so strong it both thrilled and frightened her. At times it even threatened to overwhelm her.

Desiree knew she would never experience that extreme level of passion again. What troubled her was that she couldn't be sure what she felt for this loss. Relief - or regret?

Chapter Two

Hans Faber stood on the balcony of his flat, gazing down at the bustling streets below as he nursed his cognac. Like the cunning hawk he was, he had spent the better part of the last two weeks learning as much as he could about his prey. He knew Desiree's daily habits, her weekly routine, her haunts. He knew how many men she had slept with during that time; two and how many women; one. The number seemed surprisingly low for a woman of her reputed appetites. But he had also learned that she lived her life as though she were always in search of something elusive, never able to stop and rest.

Now it was Friday; he was alone and aroused, as he had been for most of the last week. It was part of his preparation for what he was sure would be his most challenging case. He wanted to keep that edge, that raw hunger. As it had when he swum competitively as a youth, that edge kept his focus keen; his mind alert. Oh, there had been several times when he'd had to relieve himself from the discomfort. But he had denied himself any real pleasure in obtaining release. It had been quick, hard and joyless.

The joylessness was the most difficult part. Hans hadn't realized what a considerable effort it would be for him to deny himself even the most basic of sexual pleasures. He hadn't realized that he found such exhilaration in the pure physicality of sex. The touching. The tasting. The sounds and scents. That part of his life had always sustained him when times were difficult, and the cravings were deeper and more profound than he had expected.

At one point it had been too much bear. The hunger for physical contact had overwhelmed him. On that night, he had Herrmann drive him to a town at some distance from Angouleme, where he found a dark alleyway filled with the equally hungry. While Herrmann stood by the car and enjoyed a smoke, Hans disappeared into the alley and found a young man, a boy, really, eighteen at most, with dark hair and deep brown eyes, a virtual doppelganger for the woman he so desired.

A mouth is a mouth, he thought, as he watched the boy minister to his needs. Lips, teeth, tongue were all that mattered. The touch of another person. Hans let himself take pleasure this time; prolonged it, in fact; at one point even caressing the boy's soft hair. He came deep in the boy's throat, savoring each spasm. Afterward, he roughly pulled the boy up and shoved his tongue into his mouth to taste himself. Then he pulled back and struck him, hard, knocking him to the ground. As the boy gazed up at him in pained confusion, Hans drew out his wallet and tossed a few francs at his feet, then turned and strode away.

That had been Wednesday. Now it was Friday, and the hunger was back in full force. Tomorrow, he would make his first move in the labyrinthine plot he had devised to capture his prey, seduce her, and unleash that passion he craved from her.

***

That very same Friday night, Desiree was in the town Hans had visited that Wednesday. She was seated at a small café with a young married couple, and the three were flirting. Desiree had little interest in Guillaume. She had long outgrown boyish men. But he was part of the package that came with Marie, a tender young blonde whose endearing shyness captivated her; at least at that moment, on that night, in that week, month and year.

The three were laughing together when Desiree spotted Rene across the street. Thankfully, it appeared that he hadn't seen her. She laughed again at some particular idiocy uttered by Guillaume, and it was then that Rene turned and saw her. For a moment Desiree was sure that she had seen shock flash across his face at the sight of her with what were destined to be her companions for the night. Then a sly smile crept across his face, and he winked. Desiree smiled back at him before turning to her companions once more.

Guillaume and Marie took Desiree back to their small flat. Once inside the door, she turned to Marie and began to kiss her deeply, her tongue exploring that sweet pink mouth. Marie surprised her by returning her kisses eagerly while Guillaume caressed Desiree from behind, his erection pressed against her backside. He reached around in front of her, his hand snaking under her dress and into her panties.

Desiree moaned, and her head fell back against Guillaume's shoulder. He was young, yes, but his touch was practiced and sure. He gathered her moisture on his fingertips and stroked her bud with it, making her gasp. Marie, feeling neglected in their erotic reverie, grabbed Desiree's face and kissed her with renewed fervor. The girl hadn't realized how much she had wanted this, how much she had hidden from herself in burying the memories of those achingly electric adolescent fumblings with her best girlfriend.

Guillaume watched, eyes wide, drinking in each moment. It was a dream come true to see his pretty young wife with another woman, and he was more aroused than he had ever been in his life. He pressed closer to Desiree and drove two fingers deep inside her, reveled in the gasp he elicited from her. He then brought his glistening fingers up and stroked them alongside those kissing lips, painting the very corner of each woman's mouth. They broke their kiss then, and each mouth engulfed a finger and sucked the moisture from it, their hands caressing each other feverishly.

With one swift move Guillaume pulled up Desiree's dress, yanked down her panties and drove himself deep inside her. He held himself very still as she cried out and pulsed around him. Marie slid down Desiree to her knees, trailed her hands up the woman's quivering thighs and swiftly buried her mouth between her legs.

Six a.m. Desiree awoke in the couple's wide, white bed, the two of them asleep in an embrace beside her. She slid carefully out from between the sheets, dressed and slipped out of the flat. She walked back to the café where her truck was parked, hopped in and began the drive home.

It was better this way; to disappear from these people's lives like a wraith in the night. That way, no one was hurt, and if they wished, Marie and Guillaume could think of last night as nothing more than a dream.

***

Six a.m. Hans was awake, alert, staring at the ceiling. He had dreamt about Desiree all night, dreams so vivid that he imagined he could still feel the press of her flesh against his. Her imagined scent was in his nostrils, her taste in his mouth. He stroked himself lazily as he thought of the night to come.

Chapter Three

Hans turned in front of the mirror, checking his dress uniform from all sides. He tugged at the hem of the tunic, straightened the belt, examined the medals carefully to ensure they were perfectly placed and properly aligned. There was nothing he disliked more than a uniform with its awards improperly placed, and he had severely dressed down more than a few junior officers for such violations.

Unlike some officers, Hans didn't leave his medals on his dress tunic between wearings, instead removing them and placing each one carefully in its case until the next occasion. Doing so meant that it took a little longer to dress for each formal event, because the medals had to be replaced carefully and aligned every time. But they retained their shine, and rarely had to be cleaned or polished.

Hans picked up his cap from the dresser and placed it carefully on his head, ensuring the proper angle and tilt. He heard Herman pull up in the car down below, quickly pulled on his freshly pressed white gloves and hurried downstairs. He was on his way to M. Charles Guidon's villa outside of town for a soiree to celebrate—what were they celebrating this time? Hans scarcely knew or cared. He'd been to many a party at Guidon's and one seemed to blend into the next. He cared even less about Guidon himself, a war profiteer and opportunist who had happily welcomed the Vichy regime.

Oh, it wasn't that he objected to the man from some high moral ground. He would have done exactly the same in Guidon's place. It was that Guidon was so vulgar, so lacking in grace. A petty, stupid man and, perhaps the worst of all crimes, a crushing bore. But the fine champagne flowed freely at his parties, and there were always plenty of beautiful and willing women to be had. It was for these very reasons that Hans had been a fixture at Guidon's parties almost from the moment he had arrived in Angouleme.

But he was attending for an entirely different reason this time. His heart pounded with the exhilaration of the beginning of the hunt. There would be little champagne consumed tonight, and no women seduced. Except, of course, for the one who was the very object of his pursuit; Desiree Mendelsohn.

***

Desiree did one last check of the boxes of produce, the baskets of bread and eggs, the wheels of Brie and Camembert. As much as she disliked Charles Guidon, his many parties paid very well indeed. They played a substantial part in her income, so she was never able to turn one down no matter how much she may have wanted to.

When Desiree arrived at Guidon's villa, Guidon's chef, Mathieu Derian, regarded the boxes with a very pleased smile. "Once again you have outdone yourself," he told Desiree. "I am very pleased." He helped her to unload them and bring them in.

"Anything to be of help to you, Mathieu," she told him with a smile. While Mathieu worked for Guidon, he was nothing like him. Tall, solid with a clean-shaven head and a dignified air, he seemed far better suited for nobility than his plump, florid-faced employer. But he could also be playful, which he demonstrated at that moment by reaching out and tousling Desiree's dark hair, as though he were contending with an unruly child. She laughed and pushed his hand away.

"You are lovelier than ever," he told her. "Tell me, why aren't we still lovers?"

"Because, mon ami, you fell in love with Marriette."

"That I did. How foolish of me."

"Not so foolish, Mathieu. You have three beautiful children."

"I can always count on you to remind me where my priorities lie," he said with a broad grin. "Now wash up, let's cook. We've a great deal to do."

Desiree washed up quickly and then began chopping the fresh carrots and celery. She enjoyed working with Mathieu. They usually worked together in a companionable silence that she found soothing. It had been many years since they had been lovers, but she would never forget those nights with Mathieu. There was always a party, always the preparation and the cooking. But after the meal had long since been served and the rest of the kitchen staff was busily washing the dishes, Mathieu would take Desiree to different parts of the villa, hidden areas that seemingly no one could find, and yet he had found them. It was in these places that he would make love to Desiree with an urgency that thrilled her; an urgency she knew was only heightened by the very real risk of being caught.

At one point Desiree had thought she would marry Mathieu, that he would be a good father to her son as well as a solid, dependable husband. But it was he who had hesitated. Not because he didn't love her, but rather because he somehow sensed she had to be free. "I could not have held onto you," he once told her. "I knew that, at some point, you would leave me. That I was not what you wanted, even if you didn't realize it yourself." So he had left her, instead, but thankfully they had remained friends.

She glanced at Mathieu at work, watched him expertly shell several oysters. Why couldn't she have been happy with him? Why did she always feel as though she were looking for something she would never find? It had been different when Sasha, her beloved son, was alive. He had given her life meaning and purpose that eased the yearning for something more. But when he had died, she had been set adrift again, sent on a journey from which she felt she would never find peace.

Was this truly freedom? If it was, why did Desiree feel so imprisoned?

***

Hours later, long after the food had been served, declared a great success and the kitchen scrubbed down by the rest of the kitchen staff, Desiree walked out on the lower terrace. It was a beautiful night, clear and almost warm, and the air seemed heavy with expectation. The light from the upper terrace spilled down around her in oddly ethereal columns, and she could hear the voices and the music upstairs and, off in the distance, the nightly chorus of the frogs and crickets. She took her cigarettes from her pocket, pulled one out and fumbled for her matches. Had she left them inside?

Desiree heard a click, and suddenly the terrace was ablaze with a new light. She found a uniformed arm extended out to her, a graceful hand holding the new source of the flame; a gold lighter engraved with the SS emblem. She looked up into the almost emerald eyes of a particularly elegant SS officer in full dress uniform. He wasn't much taller than she, and yet he seemed taller in his self-assured stance. He had dark-blonde hair with an appealing touch of grey at the temples, a strong jaw and just the touch of a cleft in his chin.

Their eyes met, and although he was Desiree's enemy, a flicker of recognition passed between them, lightning quick, yet enough to give them both pause. The officer cocked his head and nodded towards the flame and Desiree leaned forward to light her cigarette. He flicked the lighter closed and stepped forward. With a click of his heels, he gave Desiree a little bow.

"Colonel Hans Faber at your service." His French was perfect.

"Madame Desiree Mendelsohn."

"Enchante, Madame," he said, and he took her hand and kissed it. His eyes locked with hers as he did so, and his mouth lingered briefly on the back of her hand with a touch so light it was electric for them both.

Desiree felt electrified. Why was he having such an effect on her?

He straightened up and smiled at her, a warm yet mysterious smile.

"It is a beautiful night," he said, and he took a deep breath. "I find that the air is particularly invigorating on nights like this, which is why I prefer to be outside."

"But shouldn't you be upstairs, Monsieur Colonel?"

"If you please, address me as Hans. I may wear the uniform now but I am not on duty." He started towards the end of the terrace.

"Hans, I don't believe you belong down here," Desiree said quickly

He whirled around and looked at her. "And why not? Am I not Monsieur Guidon's guest?"

"That is precisely why you do not belong down here, with the kitchen help."

"If you are the kitchen help, then the kitchen is indeed blessed," Hans said with a warm smile. "Come; look at the night with me."

Desiree hesitated. Her thoughts seemed to be suddenly in a whirl, and she wasn't at all sure how to behave around this charming stranger who was, after all, a Nazi; her sworn enemy.

Hans saw her hesitation, and reached out a friendly hand. "Come. What harm can it do?"

Desiree smiled in return, but still she hesitated.

Hans didn't break his gaze. With a devilish smile, he crooked his index finger to beckon her forward. "Come."

She walked towards him slowly, and he turned around and continued to walk towards the part of the terrace that faced the woods beyond. When he'd reached the end, he stubbed out his cigarette and leaned on the railing.

It took Desiree a moment to catch up to him. She put out her own cigarette and leaned on the railing beside him.

"I love to listen to the frogs and the crickets," Desiree told Hans. "It's as though they play a symphony every night, whether or not anyone is listening, simply because they love to make music."

Hans turned to look at her with a new appreciation. "The creatures of the night," he quoted.

"What music they make," she continued.

He smiled at their shared quote from Bram Stoker's Dracula. "Madame," he said, "you are proof that what one finds downstairs is usually far more interesting than what one must tolerate upstairs."

"And you, mon Colonel," she replied saucily, "are proof that when a man wants to make love to a woman, he will say anything."

"Please, address me as Hans. If we do make love, I believe we'll want to be on a first-name basis. You call me Hans, and I shall call you Desiree, which is such a beautiful name, after all. A name meant to be whispered in bed."

He stepped closer to her, and their gazes locked once more. Desiree noticed that his eyes were no longer the deep shade of emerald they had appeared when the two first met, but a softer, woodsy green, dotted with flecks of deep amber.

"Your eyes," she said.

"My eyes?"

"They're hazel. That's why they change color when the light is different. Sometimes they're a deep green, sometimes they're a deep brown, but normally they're a combination of the two colors, green flecked with brown. You have hazel eyes."

"Do you consider that a good thing?" Hans asked; his voice gentle.

"Yes," she said softly. "My father had hazel eyes." A sadness washed over her.

Hans saw that sadness and stepped closer still, took hold of her chin and tilted it up to him.

"Do you know what my eyes see, Desiree?" His voice was like a purr now, and his thumb lightly caressed her chin. "They see lips that want to be touched, a mouth that wants to be kissed."

With two fingers, Hans lightly traced those soft, full lips. He heard her sharp intake of breath, and a shiver ran through him. When his fingers pressed against her lower lip, Desiree's eyes closed, her head tilted back and her mouth opened slightly.

He could feed off these touches, Hans thought, gain a sustenance he'd never before experienced. It was so purely tactile. His fingertips had never felt more acutely sensitive, and his breath grew heavier with each touch. Desiree's mouth opened a little more, and suddenly her tongue darted out to touch his fingertips. With a soft groan Hans drew his hand away, cupped her chin once more, and covered her mouth with his own.

At first he let his lips brush lightly against hers, felt her tremble in response. Then he began to kiss her fully, his lips exploring hers with soft nibbles. He let go of her chin and drew her close to him, letting his body mold to hers, kissing her more deeply, more hungrily, caressing her lips with his own, nipping at them, finally sliding his tongue into her mouth to meet hers. He could feel her getting lost in that kiss, pulling him with her into a maelstrom of passion that thrilled him to the very fiber of his being.

Gott im Himmel. Hans felt it would kill him to break this kiss, but he knew he must. He couldn't allow the hunter to be overpowered by his prey. So, as difficult as it was, he drew back from that delicious mouth, that warm, eager body that clung so closely to his. Shivering with desire, his breath heavy, he looked at Desiree. Her face was filled with dazed bewilderment, her rich dark eyes slightly hurt, and Hans felt a sudden sharp pang deep inside him. She had given herself so willingly, so openly to him.

He took hold of her shoulders, looked straight into her eyes. "I must leave now," he told her.

"No. Don't go."

"I must. I promise you we will see each other again. Soon. Very, very soon."

He hesitated, and then planted one more deep kiss on her lips, before tearing himself away and disappearing into the night.

He left Desiree aching, aroused, trembling violently with desire, and yearning for much, much more.

Chapter Four

Hermann brought the staff car down the long drive towards the villa's high stone gates. Hans sat quietly in the back, still trying to catch his breath. He held a hand out before him and saw that he was still trembling. He was also achingly erect, but it was much more than that which had him so shaken. His body hungered for Desiree and it was all he could do to keep himself from ordering Hermann to turn the car around.

It was too much this time. He had held her, touched her, kissed her. And if he couldn't have her, he would have to find relief in another woman's body. He leaned forward.

"Take me to Madame Henriette's," he told Hermann.

***

It had been a long day, and Mathieu was finally relaxing, enjoying a late night cup of espresso. He smiled as he thought of Desiree at work that afternoon, wielding a knife almost as large as her to expertly slice and chop. She could easily have been a chef herself. Together, the two of them might have been able to build quite a successful business. A restaurant, catering—of course, it would never happen now.

Desiree burst into the kitchen, her face flushed, breathing hard, dark eyes wild and fiery. Mathieu stood up.

"Mon Dieu—what is it?"

She stood still, gazed into his eyes, breath heavy yet even. All Mathieu could hear were those soft intakes of breath.

Then he saw it. That glimmer of desire in her eyes, one that had once been so familiar to him.

"Non, Desiree," he said firmly, with far more conviction than he felt. He was already hard, just from that lustful gaze of hers.

Desiree was in front of him almost in an instant, her hands around his face, trying to pull him down into a kiss.

"Non," he said again. He took hold of her hands and brought them away from his face. "Don't do this, Desiree."

"Please Mathieu…" that voice, husky with need, set a fire inside Mathieu. He let go of her hands and backed away from her. "I beg of you. Don't do this," he pleaded.

But she had seen his arousal, and God, her eyes only made him harder. She closed the distance between them once more, fell slowly to her knees, and began to nuzzle his erection.

"Don't," Mathieu gasped, but she was already unbuckling his belt, undoing his trousers. She drew him out and took his hot, hard length into her mouth. A shuddering groan escaped Mathieu's lips. He looked down and caught a glint of triumph in her eyes. Suddenly he found himself full of rage, a rage so strong and so deep that it overpowered him, fueling his lust further.

If this was what she wanted from him, so be it, he thought. He pulled out of her mouth, roughly lifted her up and pushed her back onto the prep table. He pulled her legs over his shoulders. He didn't bother to remove her underwear. He pulled it to one side and thrust deep inside her.

She was so wet, so ready for him, the way she always had been. He held still for a moment, struggling to contain his release. Then he grabbed her legs, gripping them hard to brace himself and thrust into her, hard and fast and deep, again and again, until she cried out and came. When he felt her clutching him inside he shoved in one last time and groaned as he unleashed his seed.

***

Mathieu watched Desiree silently pack her knives, his body and soul drained, his mind and heart in a whirlwind.

"Why, Desiree? Why did you do this? You know I love Mariette."

"It wasn't as though I put a gun to your head," she replied, her voice resigned. "You wanted it as much as I did."

Mathieu jumped up and grabbed her by the arm. Desiree winced in pain but he didn't let her go. "Not like that," he told her. "Not with such rage. I wanted to hurt you. I've never wanted to hurt a woman before."

"You're hurting me now," she whispered, tears filling her eyes. He let go of her arm. What in God's name was she bringing out of him? What dark side of him had she unleashed?

Desiree looked sadly at the man who had been so good to her over the years. Without Mathieu, she would never have had the opportunity to cater Guidon's frequent parties, and many others as well. Much more important, he had been a strong, reliable and loyal friend to her.

"You didn't really hurt me. You gave me something I needed," Desiree said, but her voice was weak and unconvincing.

"I gave to you?" Mathieu shouted, once again gripping her arm. "I didn't give you anything. You took from me, without considering the consequences. Why? Why would you do such a thing?"

Desiree blinked back tears. "I don't know," she whispered. "I don't understand it any more than you do." She truly didn't. It had seemed right at the moment; and now it was so obviously very, very wrong.

Mathieu sighed and let go of her arm once more. He leaned back against the prep table with a deep sigh.

"Then I suggest, mon Cherie, that you find out why you seem so compelled to leave destruction in your wake—especially to those who care for you."

***

Hans lay still in the wide white bed, gazing dispassionately up at the young woman who rode him so vigorously. Her youth, her slim hips, her pert breasts should have been enough to carry him over into the bliss of orgasm, yet they weren't. Oh, his body responded to her slick tightness. He was very, very hard, but his mind was disengaged from all of it. Somehow a key pleasure point in his psyche remained untouched.

Hans closed his eyes to block out all but the purely physical sensation, only to have his mind flooded with images of Desiree. Her mouth against his, their tongues touching. The soft crush of her full breasts against his chest; her womanly curves in his arms. Her warm, peach-like scent. Those sweet little moans that passed from her lips to his. All converged together to bring him close, so close…

A mouth that stung with a day's worth of whiskey pressed against his, and an ashen-tasting tongue slid between his lips. Hans's eyes whipped open to confront the drunken stare of the whore.

"Nein," he growled, pushing her back. He reached up a hand and slapped her, hard. A trickle of blood spilt from the corner of her mouth, and the sight of that blood set Hans on fire. He pulled the whore down to him and licked off that blood, then flung her off him, roughly turning her face down and flat on her stomach. He lifted her hips and drove into her from behind, then stretched along the length of her body, crushing her under his weight, fingers digging into her hips in a bruising grip, holding her up to meet each violent thrust.

Hans could feel himself hitting the mouth of her womb, heard her whimper in pain; which only heightened his excitement. He could smell the blood still leaking from the corner of her mouth. He brought one hand up to grab her brittle, bleached hair and pulled her head back so he could once again taste that blood. When the rich, iron-like flavor penetrated his tongue, he drove deep into her one last time and came with a long, loud groan.

***

"This can't happen again, Hans," Madame Henriette told him as he buckled the belt on his dress uniform. He glanced back at the huddled, weeping figure on the bed. He felt nothing; no sympathy, no concern. She had been a body, nothing more, a mere receptacle for his lust. He pulled out his wallet and counted out several francs.

"You needn't worry," he told Henriette. "I won't be back." He handed her the wad of francs. "Something extra for her and for you, for all your trouble."

Henriette took the pile of francs and looked at them, considered what it would mean to lose one of her highest-paying clients.

"Let's not be hasty," she told him, trying to hand back a few - very few - of the notes. "After all, you've never gone this far before. I'm sure it was a mere aberration."

Hans pushed aside the proffered notes and looked deeply into Henriette's eyes, watched her back away from his cold, steely gaze.

"Have you not yet realized it?" he said. "I am the aberration."

And with a last tip of his cap, he left.

Chapter Five

It had been two weeks, and still Desiree hadn't heard from Mathieu. She knew Guidon had a dinner party planned for the end of the month, and if she didn't hear from Mathieu soon, she wouldn't be able to get the goods needed for it.

Desiree had resigned herself to the loss of Mathieu's presence. After all, her entire life had been a series of losses, beginning with the death of her parents when she was still a child. But she hadn't realized how much she would miss Mathieu. It wasn't just that she'd come to rely on him for a portion of her livelihood. It was the man himself, who he was and how he had always cared for her. Mathieu knew her better than anyone else in the world, and Desiree dreaded the idea of life without him.

But she did what she knew best; took on that coping mechanism that had helped her through every other loss in her life. She cut off that part of herself, severed the nerve endings and put it into a box, and then she put that box in another box, and then that box in another box until all the feelings were well hidden and completely insulated. It was the only way Desiree knew how to cope with a loss, and it had always worked.

She had other, more important things to think about. She had just returned from her last run and had no idea where she was going to hide the sheaf of American dollars Guy had given her. For the time being she had spread them out within the lining of her thick jacket, but she certainly couldn't keep them there.

What on earth had Guy been thinking? Usually when Desiree made one of her "special" deliveries she was paid either in francs or Reichsmarks at the occupation's established exchange rate of 20 francs to one Reichsmark. She knew that American dollars carried a far greater value than either, but they were also a great deal more dangerous to handle, and' unlike the latter two currencies, she couldn't count on using any of the dollars to purchase her own goods for her customers. She was lucky she still had enough left from Guidon's last party to do so, and she was just about to begin unloading her truck when she froze in her tracks.

An SS staff car was coming up the long dirt road that led to her cottage. There was no time to panic. On immediate and full alert, Desiree removed her jacket slowly and tossed it into the cab of the truck.

Desiree took a deep breath as she watched the car pull to a halt. The driver got out to open the passenger door. The officer who emerged was clad in the typical black boots, black leather trench coat and skull-marked cap. He looked vaguely familiar to her; could it be?

"Desiree!" he called out, with a wave and an eager grin. It was indeed the very same officer Desiree had met at Guidon's last party. Her heart was pounding with anticipation. Did he somehow know?

His expression turned quizzical as he approached. "Do you not remember me?"

"Yes, I do...Colonel Faber, is that right?"

"Hans," he said moving forward to grasp her hand and bring it to his mouth for a kiss. "You are as lovely as I remember."

He held on to her hand for a moment and simply looked at her; almost as though he were feasting his eyes. That appreciative gaze somehow made Desiree relax; it was obvious he wasn't there to arrest her.

"You are probably wondering why I drove all the way to your home today," he began. "First, I wanted to see you again. I would have come sooner but, alas, my work kept me away. Second, I spoke to M. Guidon's chef about you, and I wish to engage your services as a caterer for a small reception I am planning at my flat."

"Certainly, Colonel," Desiree replied, skillfully hiding any sense of relief from her voice. "Shall we go inside to discuss it?"

"First, let me and my driver assist you in unloading your truck," he turned back toward the car. "Hermann! Come here!"

"Colonel, that isn't necessary..." This time it was difficult for Desiree to hide the anxiety in her voice.

"Hans, please. I call you Desiree, you should call me Hans."

"Hans, I can unload my truck later..." Desiree fought the desperation inside her.

"No, no, I insist that we help." The gate had already been pulled down, so Hans reached in and began sliding out a large box of tomatoes.

He handed it to Hermann. He pulled out another box of tomatoes and handed it to Desiree, then pulled out a third for himself.

"And where would you like these?"

"I have a refrigeration shack to the side there."

"Everything I have heard about your legendary produce appears to be true," Hans told Desiree as they carried them to the shack. "I have never seen such magnificent tomatoes."

"Thank you, Col—Hans." Desiree tried hard to still the shaking inside her.

Within minutes the three of them had emptied the truck. Only one last thing remained; Desiree's jacket, which lay clearly visible on the seat of the cab. Hans reached through the open door to pull it out. When he turned to give it to her, something in her expression must have changed for he hesitated, and his eyes—now a dark brown—caught and held hers, and for a moment Desiree was sure he had seen right through her.

Finally, he smiled, gently folded the jacket, and handed it to her. "Mustn't forget this," he said, "I'm sure it has proved very useful on many a cold morning."

"Monsieur Colonel…" She quickly took the jacket from him and put it over her arm. Her heart was pounding now.

"Hans, please. I should think that after our last meeting it would be much easier for you to address me by my first name," he said with a mischievous wink.

"Hans…we should go inside now to talk about your reception." It unnerved Desiree to have the jacket so close to the two of them.

Hans followed Desiree into her cottage, removing his cap. It was small and spare, yet cluttered with books and papers. Along the walls were some of the many photographs Desiree had taken over the years, including several portraits of her son at different ages, the last as a dark-eyed, brooding teenager, likely taken shortly before his death.

In one corner stood a roll top desk; equally cluttered. Hans walked casually over to the desk. He noticed what looked like a photo face down. On the back was written Mathieu - 23-7-39. He quickly turned it over to see a portrait of Guidon's chef, Derian, asleep amidst a tangle of sheets.

Hans smiled and placed the photo back face down.

He turned back to Desiree, who was still holding her jacket. He glanced down at it, then looked her straight in the eye, holding her gaze, his own unblinking and steady.

That gaze unnerved Desiree. She took the jacket and hung it quickly in her wardrobe, trying not to look at it, then turned back to Hans, gesturing toward a small table and chairs.

"Have a seat, Hans, please."

Hans placed his cap neatly on the table and sat down. He leaned forward, hands clasped together, as Desiree sat down facing him.

"Now, where were we? Ah, yes, my reception. It will be held two weeks from today and, as I said, I would like you to cater it. I have already obtained the necessary champagne. What I need is a variety of delectable hors d'oeuvres to go with it."

"How many will attend?" It was far easier for Desiree now that she was in familiar territory with him. She loved catering.

"Approximately twenty-five; give or take a few. It will take place following a meeting with members of the local high command of the occupation. The meeting will end at 5 p.m., and the reception will follow. I expect it to last for about two hours, after which we shall all depart for dinner at M. Guidon's villa. Will you be assisting in the kitchen again?"

"I wouldn't be able to do so if I am to cater your reception."

"Too bad. But I would much rather have your talents for my event."

"A variety of hors d'oeuvres for twenty-five to thirty people... beginning at 5 pm..." Desiree bent over a pad, writing it all down.

"I will pay you well. Which currency would you prefer? Francs? Reichsmarks? American dollars?"

Desiree looked up sharply, right into those eyes, now a much darker, more piercing brown. Again, he held her gaze, and again, her heart began to pound. Suddenly his eyes softened, and he reached out to take her hand.

"Are you frightened of me?"

"No," she said evenly, "I'm not." Her voice was much calmer than she felt.

"That is good. I would never wish to frighten you." He continued to hold her hand.

"Francs," she said.

"Pardon?"

"Please pay me in francs."

"Very well; we have an agreement, then." He was still holding her hand, but now his thumb began to gently stroke the inside of her wrist. Desiree caught her breath, unable to tear her eyes from the slow, seductive motion of his thumb against her pulse.

"I have thought about you often since that night," he told her in hushed tones. "In fact, there are times when I cannot stop thinking of you."

Desiree remained silent, but her heart continued to pound, and for a different reason now...

"I think of how soft your lips are, the taste of your mouth...have you thought of me?"

"Oui," she whispered. She had thought of him, as much as she hadn't wanted to.

"Pardon?"

"Oui," she said it louder this time, almost in desperation.

Hans stood up then, still holding Desiree's hand, and she stood as well. Suddenly, he pulled her to him and kissed her deeply. Desiree fell into that kiss, let him tease her with his lips and tongue, and feverishly returned it.

If he could only hold her and kiss her like this forever, Hans thought. The way she responded to him, with such heat and fervor. The softness of her body against his. The little sounds she made, those sighs and moans of pleasure, the taste of her tongue—he never wanted to let her go.

He pulled back from her delicious mouth to kiss her cheeks, her chin, her throat. He moved his lips along her jaw and up the side of her face, and when he reached her ear he stopped long enough to whisper to her that he had wanted to do this from moment he'd first seen her that day—but she wouldn't let him finish, instead she pulled him back into a kiss so passionate he was almost undone by it.

Hans let one hand drift to her breast, stroked her taut nipple with the same two fingers that had caressed her soft lips that first night. She gasped and fell back from him, put her hand over his to keep it there. He nipped at and bit her ear, his moans echoing her own.

His hand slid from her breast down to the waistband of her dungarees and slid underneath them to the soft, very wet cleft between her legs. With a sigh he stroked her there, his thumb pressed to her swollen bud, still nipping at her ear then nibbling along her face and chin. He returned to her ear once more.

"I want to taste you," he whispered, his breath hot, and his mouth quickly captured the moan that issued from her lips.

Hans continued to kiss her as he pulled down her dungarees and panties, baring her to him, and lifted her up onto the table, pushing the papers off onto the floor. He pulled the dungarees and panties completely down, then knelt between her legs, spreading her open, and dragged his tongue through her sweet nectar with a hungry groan.

He licked and licked at her, tickled and caressed her little bud with his tongue, then took it into his mouth and sucked it until she cried out and came.

He thrust two fingers into her to feel her contractions, found that exquisite pressure point inside her and began to stroke it firmly, encircling it with the very tips of his fingers until she came again, and this time her cry was long and drawn out.

Even then he didn't let up, continued to suck her tender bud and stroke her inside until she came yet again, so wonderfully, terribly open to him, so incredibly responsive to his every touch, and the feeling that rose in his throat nearly choked him. He withdrew his fingers, opened his mouth and darted his tongue into her, and sobbed against her cunt as he came without touching himself.

He leaned against her thigh afterwards, struggling to catch his breath. Then he rose over her, kissed her eager mouth and let her suck her flavor from his tongue. When he pulled back she reached up to touch the tears on his cheeks, locked her gaze on his blazing, now emerald-green eyes and the look of utter astonishment on his face.

"You've bewitched me," he breathed. "You've utterly bewitched me."

And then he captured her mouth once more with a passionate kiss.

Chapter Six

As his staff car pulled away from Desiree's cottage, Hans reflected on what had easily been one of the most intense experiences of his life—he, who had killed with his bare hands; but then, that had been an act without passion for him. This had been its polar opposite. Desiree's taste was still in his mouth, her scent on his fingers. He had always enjoyed exerting control over a woman by pleasuring her with his mouth, but this had been entirely different. He had lost himself between those soft thighs.

But Hans had a job to do; one that he was finding more and more challenging, especially now that he was virtually certain that Desiree was smuggling weapons. There had been word that a large cache of American dollars had passed through the region, which meant only one thing: weapons were being purchased. And from the way Desiree had reacted when he had deliberately mentioned paying her in such currency, and how she had held on to her jacket, he was quite sure he knew exactly where those dollars were.

Part of him felt the natural gratification of the hunter closing in on his prey. He was, after all, a detective first and foremost. He had always felt that in this role he was essentially a hunter of humans. After all, what was the end purpose of searching for and gathering evidence? To capture a human being. To do so, Hans had to know not just the habitat of his prey, but its nature as well, just like any hunter of animals.

His skills in this arena were legendary, and Hans took great pride in them. He couldn't help but be pleased now. But another part of him was deeply uneasy. It was a part of himself that he usually had no problem keeping subdued; doing so, in fact, was what fueled his sexuality, the eagerness with which he embraced the sensual, the exuberant pleasure he found in the sheer physicality of sex and the exquisite if temporary bliss of orgasm.

It was that part of Hans that hungered for something beyond himself. For as long as he could remember, he had felt alone, cut off somehow from the world and from other people. In many ways he treasured the independence that acute sense of alienation brought him. It was what made him strong, what fed his intelligence and his talents. It was so much an intrinsic part of him, who he was and always had been, that he couldn't imagine life without it.

He could barely remember when he had first become aware of this hunger. He had been very, very young; not more than six or seven. A neighboring boy, much older than he, had been the one. A boy he admired and looked up to, almost to the point of worship.

It had been worship, now that Hans thought about it. How else could he explain the sheer bliss he had felt when Friedrich had touched him in a way that was not at all innocent? Something had soared inside him at that touch. He had, after all, so very rarely been touched or held and never, ever kissed; his parents both being far too Prussian to ever show him affection.

It had only happened once. Perhaps afraid of what he'd done, Friedrich had never touched him again, not even to lay a friendly hand on his shoulder or give him an affectionate slap on the back, as he always had before. They had remained friends, but something had changed; something had been lost forever. And that was when the hunger had begun.

As Hans grew up, there had been other boys, childish fumblings, momentary bursts of heated pleasure, always leaving him yearning for more. These scattered experiences sustained him through all those lonely years spent so far away from home. He had been sent away to school when he was only eight and, even now, as he remembered it, Hans felt that sharp stab of excruciating emotional pain; the pain of rejection, of loss, a pain so unbearable that he kept it buried very deeply within him.

That pain had only fed his hunger further, creating a level of need inside him so strong and so terrifying that he quickly came to welcome the control and discipline required of his schooling. Indeed, when Hans thought about it, those two qualities had been the most valuable aspect of his education; far more valuable than the mathematics, the history, the literature, the Latin and the sports. His carefully cultivated self-control and discipline had not only helped him keep his hunger at bay, it had brought him academic and then professional success and recognition.

And yet Hans had never been able to completely deny the power and sustenance he derived from feeding that persistent hunger.

As a horseman, he understood that even the most well-trained of thoroughbreds needed time to play, to let loose all control and unleash the most feral aspects of his existence. Hans knew he was no different from that thoroughbred. There would always be times when he needed to unleash his most primitive, raw self. And for him that outlet had always been sex.

In fact, in sex Hans had found a way to link those two opposing sides of himself—the controlled, disciplined side and the raw, feral side. And he had done so from the very start with all the women—and the few men—he'd had in his adult life. He'd found that ability in his first experience with a woman, when he was sixteen. She was the mother of a school friend, and it had been one of many, many summers when his parents had left him with others, preferring to enjoy their travels on their own.

Frau Wennig had welcomed Hans into her home and into her bed. It was through her that he had learned that control could be used in other ways; to give pleasure, to prolong it, for himself and for his partner. Frau Wennig had given him something much more important, however; she had awakened his sensuality, heightened his ability to both give and find pleasure in a single touch. She had touched and kissed every part of his body, almost reverently, bringing the boy who had craved physical contact an ecstasy so exquisite that it had left him breathless. She was the one who had made it possible for Hans to unleash his hunger and revel in it.

But she had not taught him how to still the hunger, and Hans had always worried that, as much as it enriched him, it might someday overtake him and be his undoing. And at no other time had he felt this more strongly than with Desiree. He felt he was losing himself in this woman. The way she responded to him, the thrill of that response, the fire she had lit inside him. The way her eyes met his and held them…

Hans sat up straight. He had just realized something. He understood now why Desiree had seemed so familiar to him from the moment he'd first seen her photo. He knew why that flicker of recognition had passed between them the night they first met. It was because this woman shared his hunger.

At long last Hans had met his match. He had captured the one prey he wanted to keep; and he couldn't.

***

Desiree sat at her table, deeply troubled. This man, this SS officer, had given her such exquisite pleasure that she was still trembling. Now that he was gone, she was yearning for him. Whenever she had yearned for a man it had led to trouble, but this man brought much more than trouble. He brought genuine danger, not just to her, but also to many, many others.

That part of Desiree that welcomed such danger felt an odd sense of exhilaration that had always made it possible for her to take risks. She had felt it with Mathieu, in all those hidden alcoves in Guidon's villa. She felt it every time she made one of her "special" runs. And she had felt it from the moment she had first met Hans, first seen the SS emblem engraved on his lighter.

Desiree knew what that emblem meant, what his uniform symbolized. Intellectually she found it repellent; a symbol of the basest instincts of what had once been her people. But another part of her had always secretly been thrilled by it; indeed, by all of the uniforms of the occupying forces. They brought back distant memories of her dead father, and the uniform he had worn so proudly in the Great War. He had survived all four years, only to be cut down, with her mother, in the great flu epidemic.

A microscopic organism had managed to do what all the great guns on the Western Front could not and, in doing so, had left a permanent gulf in Desiree's heart. Throughout her life she had tried to fill that gulf without success. Sex had certainly been one way, from her first encounters with girls when away at school to her first, ultimately successful, attempt to seduce one of her university professors. But sex had also brought with it a sense of joy and exhilaration somehow unobtainable in any other part of her life.

Until the birth of Sasha. He had been a gift, the one person in the world who truly loved her and did so without reservation. He had given her life direction, taken her out of her self-inflicted solitary and forced her to focus on someone outside herself. His death had been sheer agony, as though a limb had been torn from her. A tearing, wrenching pain unlike any she'd ever known. Desiree had come very close to losing her sanity then. Had it not been for Mathieu, Mariette and Rene, she very likely would have.

Somehow she had survived that loss. But it had left the gulf in her heart a great deal wider and deeper than before. Only one person had been able to bring her back from what had become a living death, and he had come from the most unexpected of places.

She had caught Uwe's eye the moment she first entered the camp. He had been among the most notorious of the SS guards, a man known and feared for his abject cruelty, which could be both random and calculated. One never knew which, and that only made him more feared. But with Desiree he had been kind, almost tender. He gave her the sense that she was somehow treasured, a very precious gem to him.

It was only in bed that his dark side came out. He would bite her, scratch her, slap her, bruise her and Desiree had responded to all of it, experiencing an ecstasy so powerful there were times when she felt as though she had left her body completely. Yet that part had not surprised her. She had always wanted to completely let go of herself.

No, what had surprised her was how willingly she would trade places with Uwe, finding great pleasure in treating him just as roughly as he treated her, eliciting the very same cries of intense pleasure from him that he had brought out of her.

But there had been one night when all of that had changed. Desiree had been on top of Uwe, very close to coming, when she lifted her hand to strike him, but this time he caught her wrist, stopping her.

"No more," he had hissed. "No more. Enough."

He had pulled her off him, pushed her away, and turned away from her. There had been silence then, broken only by Desiree's soft intakes of breath. Finally, Uwe had spoken.

"I will not allow you to debase yourself any further," he had said, his voice quiet yet firm.

"I am in love with you," he told her then. "More in love with you than you will ever know or understand. I wanted you to love me, but that cannot happen."

Desiree had tried to reach out to him then, but again he had pushed her away. He rose and began to dress, tossing her camp uniform to her.

"I will not let it happen," he had continued. "It is because I love you that I will not let it happen.

"I will arrange for your freedom. I will almost certainly be sent to the eastern front for doing so. But I must do this for you and, in a sense, for myself as well. It may be the only way I can redeem myself."

They had both finished dressing, and Uwe had turned back to look at Desiree once more, his large blue eyes glistening with unshed tears.

He had reached out then, touched her cheek, caressed it. He gave her a sad smile.

"I will free you," he whispered. Then he had once more put on the mask of the camp guard, pulled her out of the small hut they had been in and brought her back to her barracks.

Desiree never saw Uwe again. But within a week, she was indeed free. Just as he had always done everything he had ever said he would do for her, Uwe had made that one last thing happen. It was the most important gift he could give her; her life. Months later she found out he had died on the eastern front.

She had not been able to weep for him. She had never been able to weep for anyone except her beloved son. But now, remembering Uwe, she thought of Hans. She thought of the fierce passion she felt for this man she barely knew, a passion she felt compelled to pursue, regardless of the cost. She needed that passion as much as she needed air to breathe, regardless of the risk and the danger.

And with that knowledge, Desiree lay her head down on the table and began to weep.

Chapter Seven

Hans held the boy by his slender throat, pushing his face into the hard brick wall. His other hand gripped the boy's hip and held him steady for each hard thrust. His mind was on fire, every one of his senses fully attuned to this very moment, the heat and the rage and the pleasure of it, the aching, desperate need for release running headlong against the equally strong desire to prolong the physical pleasure; to lose himself in it until the sharp, lightning-like bolts of completion overtook him.

He pulled the boy's head back, slowing his thrusts to savor the slick slide along that tight channel, letting his tongue snake along the boy's ear, reaching around to grab and then tug at the boy's stiff cock, thumb sweeping through the secretions on the sensitive head as he nipped and bit at that tender ear. The boy's whimpering thrilled Hans, spurred him to move faster, harder, until the slap of flesh on flesh seemed almost deafening. But then, that sound, and others similar to it, permeated the dark alleyway, the thick air punctuated by moans, gasps and growls.

The boy stiffened against him, and Hans opened his hand to catch the turgid spills, feeling the boy's inner core clench and release, clench and release until it pulled his own seed from him so forcefully that he bit down into the boy's shoulder, hard, to stifle his sharp cry of release.

He slumped against the boy then, panting hard, and brought his spunk-filled hand to the boy's mouth, shivered as he felt the tongue against his palm, lapping up every last drop. He surprised himself then by kissing the boy's ear, then gently licking the sweat on the back of his soft neck, just beneath his downy curls of dark hair, luxuriating in the sensation of his whole being now beautifully satiated, however brief that sensation might be.

Hans surprised himself again by wrapping his arms around the boy, gathering him closer in an embrace almost tender. He felt the boy settle back into that embrace, and remembered himself at that age; so starved for physical contact that he would have done anything to have someone, man or woman, embrace him in this way. Had he known at that age that such dark alleyways existed, he might very well have been exactly like that boy, seeking them out for whatever physical contact he could find.

He had been thinking a great deal lately of the boy he once was. He had been so vulnerable then, so hungry and needy. Since meeting Desiree he had the sense that this same boy was being aroused from a deep slumber. Elements of himself that hadn't felt anything in so long were now full of feeling. Part of Hans was exhilarated by it, but another part was terrified. After all, with feeling came the risk of losing control; something Hans feared as much as he yearned for.

Hans let the boy go, pulled out of him and drew up his trousers, watching the boy do the same. The boy turned and looked at him with those large, shining brown eyes; the ones that reminded him so much of Desiree. The look on the boy's face was luminous, almost beatific, and that look tore at him, filled him with anger and despair. He grabbed the boy by the neck with both hands, pushed him back into wall.

"Never, ever, look at me that way," he growled. He watched as tears welled up in the boy's dark eyes, then let him go. With a sigh, he drew out his wallet, pulled out several francs and held them out to the boy, who shook his head. Hans shoved the notes into the pocket of the boy's jacket. He was about to leave when he hesitated, looked once more at this boy whose hunger reflected his own. He saw himself at that age, eyes wide with need. With a sad smile, Hans reached out and touched the boy's cheek, lightly, almost tenderly, then turned and left.

Hans realized, as Hermann drove him back to Angouleme, that the sex had been nothing more than a brief palliative. The ache was still there. No matter what he did to try to obliterate it, it stayed with him, filling his senses with raw need. It was almost more than he could bear.

Hans sat back and took a deep breath. He concentrated hard, tried to push back the need. Focus and control. Those were his bywords, and they had never been more important to him than they were now. He had a job to do, and that job came first and foremost. Whatever he felt for, wanted of Desiree, it had to be directed by his mission and purpose, especially since he was so close to his objective.

And yet, and yet it was nearly impossible to do so when every time Hans closed his eyes he could smell her, feel her soft skin, hear the tiny sounds that erupted from her throat when he touched her. And her taste, her sweet, sweet taste, lingered on his tongue.

Hans opened his eyes, shook his head. Control. How desperately he needed it, now more than ever before, now, just as he was beginning to feel it slip through his fingers. A part of his psyche grabbed at it, clutched it tight to his heart, hoping to still the ache, the yearning, the very rawness of it. Hans was not a man who feared much in life. He had killed, after all. He had taken human lives. And not just with guns but also with his bare hands.

He had once choked the life out of a man. While the act itself had been almost dispassionate, Hans remembered how, at the very moment he felt the man's life slip away, he had been filled with a sense of power and omnipotence he had never before experienced. After all, at that moment he had never been more in control. And at that moment the wounded child inside of him had arisen and pushed back all barriers to stand tall before curling into himself once more to disappear into the depths of Hans's psyche.

The immense pleasure, psychologically and, he had to admit, emotionally as well as physically, that he had already experienced with Desiree had awoken that boy once more, and now he refused to fall back into slumber. Keeping that boy buried deep inside him was what had kept Hans so strong throughout his life, and he feared losing that strength.

But to be so raw, so open, so vulnerable and, consequently, so very much alive was almost dizzying. There was something very powerful in all that feeling. If he could harness that power and use it to his advantage, redirect it toward his goal, he could that much more effectively capture his prey and yet keep himself safe.

That was exactly what he would do, Hans decided. He would use that power to both captivate and capture Desiree, while allowing them to unleash and explore their shared hunger - together.

***

Desiree was worried. She had been carrying the American dollars for five days now and still hadn't received any word on what to do with it. She knew that the longer she held that money, the greater the danger to herself and others. She had heard through the grapevine that the occupation was aware a large cache of American dollars had entered the region, so she knew her contacts were lying low for the time being. She just wished someone would come and relieve her of at least some of the bills and therefore increase her odds for safety. But there was nothing she could do about it except wait.

The phone rang, startling Desiree. Wonder of wonders, it was Mathieu.

"I have not called you," he told her, "because I wanted to think, to make sense out of what happened between us."

"Mathieu...I'm so sorry..." her voice broke, and the tears flowed. Tears of regret for what had happened, and of relief that her dearest friend had not abandoned her after all.

"Non, mon Cherie. It was as much my fault as yours. You didn't take a pistol and hold it to my head, after all. Had I not wanted it, I wouldn't have become as aroused as I did."

"I shouldn't have tempted you so."

"You did what you did, and it's over with. We were both weak. We each gave in to that weakness and shared a moment together. We mustn't let it destroy our friendship."

"I felt so horrible about hurting you."

"You didn't hurt me, and you mustn't think that you did. You mustn't punish yourself. I think, sometimes, that you feel you need to be punished in some way for some unknown transgression. You don't, and you must stop thinking that way."

"You forgive me, then?"

"There's nothing to forgive. You taught me how to love. You made it possible for me to love. I would not be as happy as I am now with Mariette and our children if not for you. I only hope that you, too, can someday find such happiness."

At that moment Desiree longed to share with Mathieu everything that was going on in her life; the dollars, Hans, the terrible risks she had been taking and would continue to take. But she couldn't endanger her dearest friend and his family.

"My other reason for calling is to ask you if you'd heard from an SS Colonel named Faber. He was at Guidon's last party and, the next day he came back to the house to speak to me about you. He wanted you to cater a small soiree for him."

"Oui, I did hear from him, and I will be catering that soiree. Thank you for referring him to me."

"I'm glad that I could help. But Desiree, be careful around this Colonel Faber. He's not your average occupation functionary. He's an investigator, and, from all accounts, a very good one. An officer of his ranking and responsibility doesn't show up in a small village like Angouleme without a reason."

A chill ran through Desiree at those words, and, in that instant, she knew why.

Desiree's world once again came crashing down around her. When she'd hung up the phone, she sat down at her kitchen table to think. Of course. It all made sense. His appearance on the balcony that night, his timely visit when she'd returned from her last run. He must have known that she had the American dollars. But why hadn't he arrested her? And why had he seduced her, given her such a particularly intimate pleasure, and with such passion?

Perhaps it was just part of his methodology. Yet he had seemed so undone by it. Desiree knew he'd also experienced physical pleasure from the act. And the way he had looked at her afterwards, his eyes so full of wonder. Had it all been just an act?

Desiree was determined to find out. She had an appointment in Colonel Faber's offices the very next day to review the menus for his soiree. If seduction was simply a part of the investigative process for him, he'd soon find out that two could play at that game.

***

When Desiree arrived in his offices the next day, Hans was completely unprepared for the flood of feeling that washed over him just at the sight of her. He pushed it back, however, determined not to lose himself in her the way he had the last time he'd seen her.

"How delightful it is to see you again," he told her, keeping himself calm, cool and collected as he spoke. "And how very, very lovely you look." He took her hand and kissed it, letting his lips linger there, smiling at the shiver that ran through her, while suppressing his own.

"Have a seat," he told her. "I have been looking forward to seeing what you've been planning for my little soiree. Hermann, I don't wish to be disturbed while I meet with Mme. Mendelsohn. See to it that I'm not."

"Jawohl, Standartenführer."

Desiree, determined to keep things business-like, spread three menus out before him, all written in her elegant hand. Her hands themselves were small, graceful and neat, and Hans couldn't help but think of how they would feel touching him…

"Brie and Reblochon with freshly baked baguette slices, green apple wedges and red grapes...smoked oysters...salmon bites in a light puff pastry...Prosciutto con melone on a thin water cracker..." Desiree recited in a clear, level voice.

She continued to review the menus, but Hans could barely hear her. Desire had flooded his senses once more. He wanted to push the piles of paper from his desk and take her, right there. He wanted to be inside her, to feel her legs wrapped around him...

He beat back those thoughts, brought himself to reality once more, picking up the menus to review them each individually. "You've done very well," he told her. "These all sound exquisite. I'll leave it up to you to select the very best. At what time will you arrive on Saturday?"

He looked up from the menus and his eyes instantly locked with hers. Desire was writ large in those dark, intelligent eyes, a desire that so clearly mirrored his own that his breath caught in his throat.

Control, he thought. Take that desire; use it. Gott im Himmel, those beautiful eyes of hers! Use that desire, Hans, he told himself. Use it.

"We are done with the menus, I think," he said finally.

"Yes," Desiree answered, her voice soft, almost a whisper. She was breathing as deeply as he was. She had lost any sense of self-control, and she didn't care.

"I think," he went on, "that we want, no, need, to touch each other now."

"Yes." Desiree said it quietly but firmly. In a sense, she had already surrendered to him.

They both rose then, met halfway around the desk in a crushing embrace, mouths locked, tongues exploring. It was exhilarating and dizzying and madly, madly passionate all at once, and Hans let himself fall into it, telling himself it was just for one precious minute so he could taste her, feel the heat of her desire. He drew her towards his chair, fell back in it and pulled her down on top of him, kissed her deeply, exulting in the sheer deliciousness of it.

When Hans finally pulled back to gaze into those large, dark eyes once more, the raw need he saw there sent another sharp pang through him. How very, very much like him she was, and how much more desirable that made her to him. How he ached for her. A chill ran through him when he realized suddenly that he had to use to his advantage so much of the precious common bond they shared. He groaned then, in both desire and despair, kissed her cheeks and her throat before returning to her lips for another impassioned exploration. He was by now very aroused, and he pressed up against her so that she could feel the acute affect she had on him.

A soft moan escaped Desiree as she rubbed back against him. He brought a hand up quickly to her mouth, covering it.

"Shhh…" he whispered, glancing at the closed but unlocked door. That seemed to excite her. She buried her face in his neck and breathed him in, while grinding against him, which made Hans shudder with pleasure.

He slipped a hand under her sweater, brought it up to her breast, and caressed her nipple through her bra until he felt it tighten and grow, straining against the cloth. Hans ached to kiss that nipple, to run his tongue around it. Instead, he slid his hand underneath the soft silk, grasped her breast and let his thumb draw circles slowly and purposefully around that hard yet tender nipple while his tongue sought hers once more.

Desiree gasped against his mouth, and her hand slid down between them to grasp him firmly. It was his turn to stifle a pleasure filled gasp as she gently but firmly stroked him through the trousers of his uniform.

Hans brought his one free hand up to her mouth and pressed his index finger against her lips. "We'll have to be quiet," he whispered, "very quiet." He reached for his belt, undid it, and began opening his trousers.

Within minutes she had mounted him, and was sliding slowly and wetly on him. As exquisite as it was, Hans held back, focused instead on what subtle movement of his hips would most effectively touch that special pleasure point he had teased with his fingers on that day in her cottage.

The hand that had lingered on her breast moved down now between them, and with three well-practiced fingers he began massaging her tender bud. Desiree gasped aloud and Hans tightened his hand around her mouth to stifle that gasp.

Hans leaned his head back slightly and closed his eyes, letting himself luxuriate in each warm, wet pull and thrust. He opened them once more when Desiree began steadily gasping behind his hand, and he made his thrusts more pointed and direct. She met each one as she raised and lowered herself on him.

Hans opened his eyes again and gazed intently at her face as she climbed towards her climax. Desiree was clutching him so tightly now inside that his thrusts had been reduced to a mere twitch of his hips, each still pointedly measured to give her the most pleasure possible. His fingers rang against her clit and he felt it retreat from him. He knew she was very, very close now.

Hans clamped his hand even more tightly around Desiree's mouth to stifle her sharp cry of release. It was all he could do to keep from joining her when he felt her strong, rhythmic clutching around him. He pulled her mouth back down to his, then, and slid his tongue inside, rolling and entwining it with hers.

This time, Desiree stifled her cry herself, by pulling away and sinking her teeth into the rough cloth of his uniformed shoulder, gnawing and chewing at it until a third climax overtook her, one even more powerful than the first two.

As the spasms inside her subsided, Desiree rested her head on Hans's shoulder. He found himself tenderly stroking her hair and kissing her cheek.

And then Hans was taken by complete surprise when, in one swift movement, Desiree lifted off his still very hard cock and fell to her knees before him, taking him deep into her throat.

Hans gasped aloud, then bit into his fist as he struggled to hold back. He felt her throat muscles ripple around him, and he gritted his teeth. He held on for dear life as she slowly slid back until only the head remained within her mouth. Hans gazed down at her and moaned softly at the sight of those soft, full lips gliding along his shaft.

Desiree began to tease the head then, caressing it with her tongue, pushing the foreskin down with her lips to press her tongue against the tender underside, eliciting a litany of soft, low moans.

Hans continued to moan as his head fell back and his mouth went slack with pleasure. He let himself be overcome by every sweetly sharp pang of pleasure that swept through him. He brought his hands down to caress her hair, then took hold of her head and gently thrust himself in and out of that beautiful mouth.

It had been building and building, but when Hans's release finally burst forth it was so intensely and exquisitely sharp that Desiree had to clamp her hand over his mouth to stifle his cry of pleasure.

Desiree continued to hold him in her mouth as he wilted, finally letting him drop from her lips. She gently drew his foreskin back over the head and planted several tender kisses along the now-softened shaft.

Hans wanted to pull Desiree up and hold her and kiss her, but she drew away from him then. Without a word she got up, retrieved and pulled on her panties and straightened her clothing. She drew her compact and lipstick from her purse, powdered her nose and refreshed her lip color. Hans watched her, dumbfounded, then stood up and began to redo his trousers.

Desiree turned back to Hans and faced him, saw the bewilderment and, could it be, hurt in his eyes. She had planned to say something cold and nonchalant, but the words wouldn't come.

"I think we both enjoyed that, Monsieur Colonel," Desiree said finally, her voice softer than she had wanted it to be. She hesitated for a moment. "And perhaps we both needed it as well," she finally went on. "Until next week, then. I'll arrive at 3 pm. That should give me plenty of time for preparation."

"Desiree…" His voice was as bewildered and hurt as his eyes, and she couldn't bear it. She turned away from him, opened the door to leave and closed it quietly behind her.

Chapter Eight

What on earth? Hans was literally stunned speechless. What had just happened? He could count on the fingers of one hand exactly how many times he had actually made love with another person, and, to his mind, this had clearly been one of them. His whole being still trembled with the after effects.

He had fucked women, and he had fucked men. He had even been fucked by men. Each had its unique physical and psychological gratifications, but it had been rare indeed when those gratifications were heightened by a tender response. That, to Hans, was making love. And he had felt that with Desiree.

Not that making love was the same as being in love. Hans had never considered himself to be a romantic man, although just about everyone who had ever slept with him would likely disagree with this self-assessment. Those who had experienced some tenderness from him would certainly feel that way, although to Hans, tenderness was a reflexive response, not an emotional one. It was not a feeling.

Hans didn't have feelings like that. As far as he was concerned, there wasn't a romantic bone in his body, much less a romantic thought in his head. What might appear romantic was simply charm and poise. It was knowing what a woman, or man for that matter, wanted to hear. It was knowing exactly what words and what touches would part the most intransigent of thighs.

Hans smiled. Somehow, Desiree had beaten him at his own game. He had to admit he admired that. After all, no one else ever had. And, mein Gott, it only made him want her even more. Of course she must have known this. What other reason could she have for leaving him so abruptly? But she would learn, as he had, that it wasn't as easy as she thought.

After all, just as her taste still lingered on his tongue, she now had the taste of his seed on hers. The intimacy of it excited Hans immensely. To have the sexual taste of another person become such an indelible sense memory seemed somehow not only primal, but also right and good. Perhaps this was where the only morality in life existed; in the blind justice of sex. Who knew? All Hans was certain of was that it was like the awakening of a long-lost instinct, all part of the elemental human desire to mate.

Hans chuckled. How people misinterpreted this desire, wrapping it up in the trappings of "love" and marriage, ignoring the hunger that was at its root! This was something he had never been able to ignore. It was what made him who he was, what give him strength and energy and talent. And it would, in the end, allow him to conquer Desiree.

***

At long last Desiree had her instructions. She was to take the American dollars to a distant town, roughly sixty-four kilometers away, where she would pick up the weapons and ordnance. She would then embark on a journey that would take her through several small towns, where her cargo was to be distributed at designated drop points, spreading it in small amounts throughout the region. During this mission, she would also pick up her regularly scheduled produce and other foodstuffs.

It wouldn't be a mission without risks, but Desiree welcomed the distraction. She hadn't been able to get that last image of Hans - stunned, eyes so hurt - from her mind. Was he really so vulnerable a person? Or had that also been an act? The way he had called to her when she left; the bewilderment and confusion in his voice. Every time Desiree thought of that moment, she again heard that voice in her head, and her heart ached.

She had to admit she still wanted this man, more than she had ever wanted another human being, male or female. There was a link, a connection between them that she could not ignore. But then, she had a job to do; a thought that suddenly struck Desiree as one that she surely shared with her lover/nemesis. They each had responsibilities they had to meet. She smiled as she recognized the very irony of the situation, that two such like-minded people would share responsibilities so clearly at odds with each other while wanting each other so passionately.

Desiree pulled up to Rene's restaurant to take his order. She had to be very careful around Rene. Somehow he had always been able to read her feelings, and he was sure to know something was up. She had to act as nonchalant as possible. She smiled as he approached her van, a broad grin on his face.

"I'm glad you're here early," Rene told her. "I have quite a large order for you this week."

"Large orders are, of course, my favorite," Desiree replied with a smile as she pulled out her order pad. The two worked together quickly, Rene counting off each item and the amount while Desiree quickly recorded all the information.

She noticed, however, that Rene kept looking at her, his expression both quizzical and concerned.

"What is it?" she asked finally with a nervous chuckle.

"You look different somehow," he told her. "Your eyes are different."

"They're the same eyes they've always been."

"No…they're not."

Desiree stopped writing and looked straight at Rene, whose grey eyes seemed unusually sharp. Could he possibly know?

"I've seen you like this before," he went on, "your eyes bright, your breath quick; like you're about to embark on some grand adventure."

Desiree shook her head, and bent down to her notebook once more. It was better to at least appear nonchalant.

"This wouldn't have anything to do with…"

Desiree looked up sharply. "With what?"

"No, it's not possible. It can't be."

"What?

"La Belle Fleur," Rene said suddenly, looking right at Desiree.

Desiree went pale.

"I thought so."

"Don't say any more, Rene."

"I'd like to kill Guy."

"No, Rene, it's not his fault."

"Involving a woman in something so dangerous…"

"Oh, you think a woman can't handle it? You think I can't handle it? If you knew how long…" she stopped suddenly, and looked away.

"Mon Dieu," Rene said, his eyes wide. "It's been you all along, hasn't it? From the start. Risking your life…"

Desiree didn't respond. Rene reached out, gathered a lock of her dark hair in his hand, and wrapped his fingers through it.

"Please," Desiree begged, "don't tell anyone, especially not Mathieu…"

Rene let go of her hair, took hold of her shoulders and turned her to face him. The look on his face was very grave.

"Don't worry, I won't. You know we can't speak about this. It would put both our lives at risk and others as well," he said quietly. "But you must be careful."

Desiree shook her head. "Rene…"

"I'm quite serious, Desiree. I couldn't be more serious. You have no idea of the danger you're in."

She reached up and removed his hands from her shoulders, looked at him defiantly. "You underestimate me," she told him. "You always did."

"Oh, no," Rene replied. "I know very well what you're capable of, and I always have. But I know something else, too. "

"And what's that?"

"I know how very reckless you can be, and that's what frightens me."

"I'm perfectly capable of taking care of myself. I've been doing so for more than forty years now."

"I know," said Rene. "And I know how very brave you are, too. Unfortunately, I also know that when your mind's made up, there's no talking you out of something, no matter how dangerous it might be."

Desiree grinned at him. "That's right."

"But you must remember, my sweet, what I told you before," he brought a hand up to her cheek and gently caressed it. "If you need me, I am here to help you in any way I can. Don't forget this."

Desiree covered his hand with hers and leaned into that tender caress. "I won't forget," she whispered.

***

Hans tossed in the bed sheets, suddenly restless. His dearest friend, Jürgen, was reading; his spectacles low on his nose. He peered over them to look at his old friend, who reached out a hand to caress his bare belly.

"Hungry for it again, are you?" Jürgen chuckled. "So who is it this time?"

"What do you mean?"

"Oh, come now, Hans. Don't put on that act with me. I've known you for nearly twenty years now."

Hans was silent, gazing forward, keeping his eyes away from the penetrating gaze of his friend. Over the years Jürgen had learned to read every nuance in the man's expressive face, and he knew, even if Hans himself didn't know, or rather refused to recognize it, that his dearest friend was in love again.

"So…who has besotted you this time?"

"Besotted is a good word for it," Hans replied. "That's how it fee… that's what it's like." He lay back and closed his eyes. Such bliss, he thought. Such bliss and torment.

He opened his eyes again, caught Jürgen looking at him, blue eyes sly yet warm. Jürgen was his oldest friend and, in many respects, his only friend, and perhaps the only person in the world who truly knew and understood him.

"I knew it. When you're that wild, that passionate, when you're begging me to fuck you…"

Hans reached up abruptly, grabbed Jürgen by his hair, pulled his head down to him, swatting off his spectacles.

"Ja," he said, "I've begged you to fuck me. And I'm begging you again. Do it. Fuck me." And with that Hans pulled Jürgen into a fierce kiss.

Jürgen was on top of Hans in an instant, lifting his friend's legs over his hips. A shudder ran through him as he gazed down at Hans's wanton, hungry face, felt him arch his hips, so unbelievably eager to be penetrated, to be taken. Jürgen had seen that hungry look before, and it never failed to set him on fire.

The first thrust came sharp and hard, and Hans gasped, winced in pain, but he wrapped his legs around Jürgen's back, and reached around him to cling to his shoulders, bracing himself. He needed this now, needed this invasion, that intense mixture of pain and pleasure, and he lifted his hips and arched up to meet each thrust.

"Don't' stop," he gasped, "harder…bitte…"

"Ja, as hard as you want," Jürgen breathed as his thrusts increased in speed. He reached down between them and took hold of his friend, began pulling him in time with each deep thrust.

"Harder…bitte…" Hans spoke between gritted teeth.

Jürgen leaned down and kissed Hans deeply, bit his lower lip, felt him shudder, felt the hot splashes of semen on his belly, the rhythmic clutching around his cock. He thrust in deep and held still, filling his friend with his seed, as he had so many times before, including earlier that very evening.

Afterwards, when they were once again lying side by side, Hans gazed up once more into his friend's penetrating blue eyes. If it were possible for him to love a man, he would love this one. But then, he doubted he could love anyone.

"I think, mein freund," Jürgen began, "that you need to take a good, long look at yourself. You think you can't feel. You think you don't feel. But you do. And you feel very deeply, much more than you're willing to admit."

"Shut up," Hans growled, reaching up again to grab Jürgen, this time by the throat. Jürgen wasn't having any of it, and he flung Hans's hand away.

"Oh, stop it, Hans," he said. "Don't posture with me. I haven't said anything that isn't true, and you know it. You've always known it."

"Ja," Hans finally said. "You've always been truthful with me. I don't think you're capable of being untruthful. It's not in your nature. But I…I'm not sure what the truth is any more."

Jürgen leaned back, grabbed his cigarettes, and offered one to Hans, who took it gratefully. He took one himself, waited for Hans to grab his lighter and light both cigarettes. The two then lay together in silence for a few minutes, smoking.

"I think you do know the truth, mein freund," Jürgen finally said. "You're just not willing to recognize it."

"Maybe so. All I know is that I want this woman more fiercely than I've ever wanted anyone, even." Hans stopped abruptly, afraid of saying too much, revealing too much.

Jürgen smiled. Even me, he thought. Even me. He didn't say it out loud, but he knew that was what Hans had almost said. He had always known, and he knew that Hans knew it, too.

"What will you do?" Jürgen finally asked.

"I have a job to do."

"That's never stopped you from doing what you wanted before."

"Gott im Himmel, I don't even know this woman." He stopped abruptly. He did know Desiree. Not every detail of her life, not her full history, not what she was like when she first woke up in the morning or at last lay her head down to sleep at night. Those times each day when he never failed to think about her.

And yet, somehow, he knew this woman, and she knew him. He felt as though he knew instinctively what made her angry, what made her sad, what brought her happiness. Call it fate, call it destiny, and Hans had never been one to dwell on either, which he had long considered romantic nonsense. But there was something in her that was so very like him. It was that hunger, that intense need that seemed to surround them both. It was like an immense cloak, one that, perhaps, might just save them both in this time of war.

***

In all her runs things had never gone so smoothly for Desiree. She'd brought the dollars to the drop-off point, picked up the weapons, driven from town to town distributing them, all without a hitch. Now she was on her way home. Somehow the fact that it had gone so easily was unnerving to her. And when Desiree felt this unnerved, she became restless.

She hadn't been able to get Hans out of her mind. His mouth. His hands. His scent; that wonderful mixture of fresh soap, leather and tobacco. How he felt inside her. How he felt in her mouth, her tongue pressed against him. And then there was the man himself, that curious mixture of razor-sharp intellect, supreme self-confidence and an almost hesitant tenderness. Desiree knew he was her enemy; that she was literally fighting against everything he stood for. But the man himself; somehow he existed apart from all that.

She could sense his disconnect from it all. He was not driven by ideology, but by a fierce desire to win, to conquer, to triumph. And she knew he was driven to conquer her, not just because it was his job, but also because he wanted her as much as she wanted him. He had touched her, kissed her, stroked her hair, and held her with a tenderness she never would have suspected him capable of. Every time she thought of him she hungered for him even more.

Desiree hadn't been with anyone since she'd last seen him. She hadn't been able to get him out of her head. She had to do so, somehow, and at the same time, she needed to assuage the hunger that enflamed her. She spotted a tavern ahead, pulled up and parked.

She spotted the young officer the moment she walked in, struck by the all-black uniform. He was considerably younger than she, perhaps by as much as fifteen years, but his frank appraisal of her made him seem unusually mature. His hair was slicked back; a look she had never particularly liked on a man, but somehow it went with the starched perfection of the uniform, the sharp, icy blue eyes and the almost impossibly pretty red mouth.

Again, he was her enemy, but Desiree felt a leap of excitement and daring in her heart. She had, after all, conquered Hans; she felt an equally strong pull to take her chances with this Nazi as well.

He smiled at her, a predatory smile, and Desiree found herself smiling back. She walked straight to the bar and ordered a beer, just what he was drinking.

"I'll get that, Erique," he told the bartender, in French.

She turned to look at him. "Merci, M'sieur."

"Pas de quoi." He came closer, until he was standing next to her. He leaned against the bar, and his eyes swept appreciatively over her once more.

"I do believe, Madame," he began in perfect French, "that your outfit is quite the most fetching in this room. Those dungarees suit you."

"Merci beaucoup. Your outfit's rather impressive, too," she told him, returning the flirt. "Black suits you."

He grinned at that. "What's your name?"

"Aimienne." Desiree might have enjoyed taking risks, but she wasn't foolish enough to use her real name.

"A very pretty name. And so romantic! Might one hope that, with such a name, there is a certain purpose to your visit here tonight?"

"What a clever way to put it. And the answer is yes," Desiree said, in almost a dare.

He leaned in closer, so close she could hear his breath quicken.

"That's good to know," he said in a low, husky voice, "because I find you very exciting." He brought a hand up and caressed her cheek before leaning in even closer to her.

"Would you like to get out of here," he whispered; his breath hot in her ear.

Desiree shivered, felt the sharp pang of desire run through her. "Oui," she whispered in his ear in return, before darting out her tongue to lightly touch his earlobe, feeling him shiver in response.

Without taking his eyes off her, the young officer pulled out his wallet, tossed a few francs on the bar. He gestured in a toast to her, and she did the same to him. Then they both downed their drinks. Their empty glasses hit the bar in unison, as though they were throwing down the gauntlet between them. They stared at each other for a moment, letting the raw, animal attraction grow even stronger between them.

"You haven't told me your name," Desiree finally said.

"Sturmbannführer Dieter Strasser, Geheime Staatspolitzei, at your service, Madame." He clicked his heels, took hold of Desiree's wrist and planted a lingering kiss on the back of her hand, his eyes never leaving hers.

So he was one of the dreaded Gestapo. This would be quite a notch in her belt, thought Desiree.

He let go of her hand, rose up, took hold of her elbow and steered Desiree swiftly out of the tavern and into the street.

"I have a room near here," he told her, pulling her briskly alongside him.

Desiree hurried to keep up with him. Her heart was pounding in her chest, prompted by the heady mixture of fear and arousal at the risk she was taking.

Suddenly the Sturmbannführer pulled her into an alleyway and into his arms, kissing her so passionately he took her breath away. An image of Hans flashed into her mind then, and she was taken back to that day in her cottage, when he had first kissed her just like this.

With that thought, Desiree returned the young officer's kiss with equal fervor, pressing up against his arousal, so hungry and eager to relive those moments with Hans. Whatever the risk, she would have this man. She had to. At that moment, she needed him.

He let her go, pulled her the rest of the distance, taking her through a separate entrance into a small boarding house. He led her down a long hallway, took out the key to open the door to his room and pulled her in after him.

He immediately began to undress, removing his waist belt, undoing the buttons on his jacket and then his shirt. Desiree followed suit, unbuttoning her sweater, pulling it off, removing her oxfords and dungarees. They never took their eyes off each other as they undressed quickly.

Without his uniform he looked frail and vulnerable, his body slender, the skin as pallid as porcelain, except for his cock, which was very, very erect, the foreskin drawn all the way back, the head ruddy. He looked strangely beautiful as he stood before her, this pale, thin creature with a hard cock, his blue eyes wild with passion, his breath a series of light pants.

He grabbed Desiree's arm, pulled her into another kiss, his tongue exploring her mouth. She felt herself being thrown back against a small bed, and he was on top of her immediately, pulling her legs over his shoulders. He took a moment to slip on a French letter before thrusting deep inside her, making her cry out from the sudden yet exquisite invasion. He fucked her hard and fast, slowing only when he felt her come.

"Ja," he breathed. "You're so hot, so tight. Do I feel good inside you?"

"Oui," she gasped, arching up against him, so hungry, so desperate for him.

He shoved deep inside her, then held still. "More? You want more?"

"Oui!" she cried, and again he fucked her hard and fast, his hips slapping against hers, until she came again. Then he began to shake and shudder, his thrusts becoming more irregular until, with a sharp cry and a final thrust deep inside, he came at the mouth of her womb.

***

Desiree woke up a while later and gazed at the young man who lay fast asleep beside her, naked and so very vulnerable-looking. He had given her what she needed, and she couldn't help but feel some affection for him. She got out of bed quietly, hoping not to disturb him, and dressed quickly. He stirred in his sleep, opened his eyes, and smiled at her.

"I enjoyed that," he said. "Did you?"

"Very much." Desiree smiled warmly at him.

"It won't happen again though, will it?"

She shook her head firmly. "No."

He smiled again, reached for his cigarettes and lit one.

"Never mind," he said without a trace of bitterness in his voice. "I'm used to it. Merci."

"Merci," she replied. She finished dressing as he watched and smoked. When she was done she went to the door to let herself out, but turned back to look at him once more.

The smile remained on his face as he took another puff from his cigarette. "Au revoir," he said finally.

"Au revoir." Desiree blew him a quick kiss then slipped out the door.

She felt renewed and invigorated as she drove her van out of the small town and headed for home. She wasn't afraid or nervous any longer. Desiree knew what she wanted, and she would take it regardless of the consequences. She hummed to herself as she drove back to Angouleme and to Hans.

Chapter Nine

It was morning, and Hans was dressing reluctantly. It had been a long time since he had seen Jürgen, and he knew it was likely to be much longer before he saw his friend again. He hated to leave, and yet, as he watched Jürgen shave at the small sink in their room, he was strangely at peace. He felt as though he knew what he needed to do in every aspect of his life, from his work to Desiree.

Jürgen finished shaving, splashed his face with water, toweled off. As he lowered the towel he caught Hans's gaze, and smiled affectionately at him. Hans had awakened him twice during the night for two more frenzied couplings. Each had been more exquisite than the last, Hans deliriously hungry and urgent in his passion, spurring Jürgen to answer that passion with his own and wringing from him two of the most intense orgasms he had ever experienced, making him, usually so quiet when he came, cry out loud from the almost unbearable pleasure.

Jürgen had awoken that morning tired yet refreshed, his limbs heavy with satiation. He would have felt at complete peace if it weren't for his upcoming parting from Hans.

"You look considerably more relaxed today than you did yesterday," he said mischievously. "Perhaps you need to be fucked more often."

Hans laughed. "There's no doubt I needed it," he replied, "but I couldn't indulge in it more often. I usually require more than two hours of sleep a night." He grinned broadly at his friend.

Jürgen buttoned up his shirt. "Have you ever stopped to think about the fact that, although you say you won't let yourself feel, that you and I have never stopped being friends all these years?"

"I know," Hans said, "and it's closer to thirty years, not just twenty."

"You're right," replied Jürgen, with a rueful smirk. "Forgive my reluctance to acknowledge how much older we've become."

Both men chuckled at that, and then each b, and possibly for a very, very long time.

"You know I'm being reassigned," Jürgen told him.

"Yes, I know," Hans said quietly. He didn't want to think of Jürgen on the Eastern Front, where his life was far more likely to be at risk. But Jürgen had chosen the Wehrmacht; had refused the SS. At heart his friend had always been an officer and a gentleman, one who preferred to lead troops into battle than engage in missions designed to bring him glory. Unlike Hans, he killed reluctantly, and he truly had no taste for that part of the job.

Hans had known Jürgen since they were both students at University. They had been roommates, and from the moment their eyes met, they became friends and were nearly inseparable.

Admittedly, they made an odd pair; Jürgen tall, dark, calm and solid; Hans short, blonde, wiry and endlessly energetic. But from the start they would spend hours just talking about their dreams, their futures, about books and women and sports. Jürgen was a star on the football field and a champion rower; Hans was a champion swimmer and accomplished horseman.

Jürgen had many friends, and Hans counted himself lucky to be among them. He had always been and always would be a loner, and to have such a devoted friend as Jürgen was a gift. Indeed, there were very, very few people he could call friends, and Jürgen was clearly the closest.

Their sexual relationship had begun as happenstance. On a Saturday night both young men had returned from their dates aroused and unsatisfied, the girls they dated consistently unyielding. And so they had turned to each other to assuage their lust. They'd each had experiences with other boys growing up, so getting a little relief from a good friend seemed entirely natural to both of them.

But from that very first night it was very clear to both of them that this was much more than two mates helping each other out. It was deliriously, intensely pleasurable, and together the two of them reached one fevered orgasm after another, all through the night and well into dawn of the next day.

That morning after, Hans had been nervous, not sure how Jürgen would react, but his good friend had acted completely naturally, and even increased his show of physical affection for his friend. In one sense, Hans was not surprised; Jürgen had always exuded an air of complete confidence, and was relaxed and calm in his masculinity.

They made love frequently after that. It was always intense, but there was also great warmth; two friends sharing their deep affection for each other. They dated women, slept with women, and continued to sleep with each other. Hans was happy for Jürgen when he fell in love with the woman who would become his wife, served as best man at his wedding, and became godfather to his eldest son. Over the years they remained close friends, and didn't hesitate to express that closeness sexually whenever possible.

Now, all these years later, Hans watched as Jürgen finished gathering his things. Then Jürgen turned to face him one last time.

"You know," he began, "my mother died when I was very young. My father hated me, blamed me for her death, and so I hated him. I didn't think I would ever love anyone."

He paused, and looked Hans straight in the eye.

"I was wrong," he continued. "I love my wife. I love my children. And I love you. I always have and I always will."

For the first time in a very, very long time, Hans was suddenly filled with a deep emotional pain. Tears stung his eyes.

"We may not see each other again for a very long time," Jürgen went on. "I just wanted you to know that, although I suspect you always have."

"Yes," Hans whispered.

Jürgen moved forward then, wrapped a hand around the back of Hans's neck and pulled him into a kiss; the first kiss they had ever shared outside of bed, the first borne of a different kind of passion the two shared.

When Jürgen pulled away, he patted Hans lightly on the cheek, smiled at him.

"It's not so bad, is it?" he said. "Loving someone—and having them love you in return."

He turned then, picked up his things and left the small room the men had shared for the last two days.

Hans sat back down on the bed. The pain rose inside him like a wave, washing over him, overwhelming him until, for the first time since he was a child, the tears began to spill. A sob escaped him, and then another, and then another.

He crawled back into the bed the two men had shared. Jürgen's scent was still in the sheets. He buried his face in those sheets and wept openly, letting all the feeling inside him cascade forth at last.

***

It was early morning when Desiree arrived home. Fighting her exhaustion, she unloaded her goods from the van and stored them carefully away in the refrigeration shed. Then, finally, the need for sleep overcame her. She fell into her bed fully clothed and pulled the coverlet over herself. Her head had barely hit the pillow when she was fast asleep.

Desiree dreamed. She dreamed of the young officer from the night before; saw the wry smile on his face, the veiled sadness in his eyes.

Suddenly he was Hans, and the sad eyes were full of tears that began coursing slowly down his cheeks. Desiree moved forward then, took his face in her hands, and began licking those tears from his cheeks. He wrapped his arms around her and pulled her close to him.

And then, just as suddenly, he was gone, and she was slapped, first on one cheek, then the other, the sting of Uwe's palm on one side, the back of his hand on the other, and once again she was filled with that mixture of fear and excitement and arousal that had marked so much of her relationship with Uwe. She was at his feet, gazing up into his face, saw the desire burning bright in his sharp blue eyes, and she nearly came at that sight—

Desiree awoke with a start. Uwe, she thought. Uwe. She knew he had loved her, but she'd refused to believe that she had loved him in return. Now, suddenly, she could feel it; feel the love she had had for him, the love she still had for him and probably always would have. And the self-loathing she'd held for this deeply suppressed love was suddenly gone.

She could think about him now, Desiree realized. She could let him back into her mind for longer than the sudden bursts of memory she'd been experiencing; bursts she had quickly smothered each time they occurred.

And suddenly it seemed very important for Desiree to do so, to let Uwe back into her consciousness, to think about and remember him. In a sense, her troubled relationship with Hans had been borne of her relationship with Uwe. Perhaps, in some way, remembering him would help her to feel whole again. Perhaps he could help her once more, just as he always had.

He had been shouting at a group of prisoners when she first saw him, urging them forward with a few sharp whips of the riding crop he always carried. He was tall, blonde, handsome. His icy blue eyes had caught hers, held them, and a curious, quizzical look crossed his face.

"Bring them here," he told the woman guard that was escorting

Desiree's group. "I need two women in Canada."

"But Oberscharführer Dichter, these were assigned to me..." the woman stuttered.

"Bring them here!!" he shouted.

The woman guard scurried to bring the group of ten women forward, and soon they were standing to attention before him. It was bitterly cold, and they tried to stand as close to each other as they could. Uwe blew on his gloved hands as he surveyed the group, his eyes flickering back to Desiree repeatedly. Finally, he pointed to a blonde woman at the other end of the line; "du" and to Desiree: "du."

"You two are very fortunate," he told them in perfect French. "You will be working with me. You'll have relatively easy duties, a little more food. And you will do exactly as I tell you. Especially when you see what happens to those who don't."

He took the two of them to Canada, named after the perceived "land of milk and honey" because it was a large barracks full of the belongings and riches of the dead. He set them to work sorting through the belongings. There were other women there, most of whom gave them no more than a passing, uninterested glance.

On that first day Uwe took Anneli, the blonde, into his office and kept her there for some time. When she finally emerged, pale and shaking, Desiree began to feel afraid.

One woman was working a little too slowly for his taste. Twice he chided her. The third time he slapped her, hard, splitting her lip. Finally, he took out his pistol and shot her in the back of the head. The two women working alongside her were tasked with dragging her body away, and they left it outside for pickup. By the time they were all excused, late that night, it was gone.

Over the next several days Desiree saw Uwe whip a woman mercilessly with his riding crop simply for breaking a porcelain plate, and shoot a man for walking too slowly. The man wasn't a part of their group, he was with another group just passing by, but Uwe shot him nevertheless.

Desiree could sense him looking at her, and she tried hard to appear blank, emotionless and unaware of all that was going on around her. She focused as much as she could on the work, but it took every effort to prevent her from trembling under the clear gaze of those blue eyes.

Finally, the day she had been dreading came.

"Du."

She stood up slowly, followed him into his office.

"Sit," he told her, closing the door behind them. She sat on one of the chairs that faced his desk. He sat behind at his desk, opened a drawer, and pulled out a pack of cigarettes, offering her one. She hesitated, but he nodded towards the pack, encouraging her. She took one reluctantly; let him light it for her.

He leaned back in his desk chair and regarded her closely as they both smoked. She tried to keep her eyes down.

"Look at me," His voice was clear, commanding.

She looked up. He was undeniably very handsome indeed; square jaw, golden blonde hair, tawny skin. That a man so physically beautiful could be capable of such cruelty amazed her; but then this war had come with many surprises.

"You're a beautiful woman," he told her. "I understand you're not a Jew. How did you come to be here? What was your crime?"

"I was accused of smuggling…" Desiree spoke hesitantly.

"Only accused? You weren't found guilty?"

Desiree fell silent. He was clever, then, she thought. That could make him more dangerous.

"I thought so. And what is your name?"

"Desiree."

"A beautiful name for a beautiful woman."

He paused then and gazed at her in frank appraisal, assessing her, his blue eyes sharp.

"I need a woman," he finally said. "For sex, yes, but my tastes are unusual. And you're the one I want."

The room was well warmed by a small space heater, but still Desiree shivered.

"Come here," he said, his voice surprisingly gentle. "I won't hurt you, and you may very well enjoy it."

Something in his voice made her shiver even more. She was aroused by that voice, by his presence, something she hadn't expected, and it disturbed her.

"Come here," he said again, and this time the command was clear.

Desiree stood up, walked towards the desk.

"No," he said, stopping her. "Here, next to me."

She walked around the desk and stood next to him. She was trembling all over now, not in fear, but in arousal, which both excited and horrified her.

He leaned back in his chair again, closed his eyes, and inhaled deeply. "I can smell you," he said, his voice husky. "I can smell your cunt."

Desiree's breath came in harsh, shaky gasps. She had never felt like this before, this heady mixture of terror and arousal, and she could feel herself growing wet. She shut her eyes, held them squeezed shut, as though by eliminating him from her sight she could eliminate his very presence.

She felt his hand move under her dress, gasped aloud when his fingers brushed along her slit, outlining it in all that wetness, then slipping inside her panties, finding her erect clit and stroking it expertly.

"Oh, yes," he breathed, his voice thick, "you like this very much, don't you? Just as I thought you would. I've chosen well, haven't I?"

And when he said that, Desiree realized that he was right, that she liked what he was doing to her, that she wanted it, maybe she'd always wanted it.

He slid two fingers inside her, brought the moisture out and spread it all around her folds. Desiree could hear the slick, slippery slide of those fingers, which only aroused her more. She moaned then, and he growled in response, grabbed her by the throat and forced her face down onto his desk, pushing up her dress and literally tearing off her underwear. She could hear him fumbling with his belt, heard the sound of his trousers fall, felt his hands on her hips, and she lifted those hips to receive him in a pose so perfectly submissive that he let out a sharp groan of desire.

And then he was inside her, filling her, and it felt right, and she moved back to meet his thrusts. "Gott," he groaned, "Das ist gut. Ja, gut."

The first smack came down hard against her right buttock, followed by a succession of hard smacks alternating between her buttocks, punctuated by an occasional pause to massage her heated skin. The smacks came harder, faster, the pain blending with the pleasure until Desiree came with a shuddering moan. He stopped spanking her then, drove into her as deep as he could and ground his hips, leaning over to cover her body.

Her buttocks felt as though they were on fire, and the burning intensified with the friction of his hips against them. And then he began nipping and biting her, all over her shoulders, her upper back and her neck, lightly at first and then more sharply as he began to thrust again.

Desiree felt as though she were drowning in a sea of sensation, coming apart somehow, losing herself in all that feeling and then she felt his hand over her mouth, and suddenly understood that he was stifling the screams she hadn't realized had been issuing from deep within her throat.

She came again, in an agony of pleasure, his teeth sunken deep into her throat. He followed shortly thereafter, driving deep inside her with a rich moan. She felt him come inside her, felt his hot semen filling her, and she came again.

And then it was quiet, with only the sounds of their harsh breathing as they both came down slowly from that pinnacle of pleasure. As she grew more conscious of her surroundings again, Desiree was suddenly aware of a steady series of soft licks against the bite marks he had left on her, and the gentle swabbing of his tongue felt soothing and somehow tender.

"I've looked for you," he whispered into Desiree's ear. "I've looked for you for so long." And he wrapped his arms under and around her and held her close to him, and she was filled with a sense of tranquility she had never known before. She knew it wasn't love that made her feel this way but something else, something very powerful she didn't understand, yet she knew she wanted more of it.

They met as often as they could after that, in his office, in an empty barracks, in a small storage shed. Each time there was pain, sometimes severe, especially when he used his riding crop against her back, her buttocks, and her thighs. He would dip it inside her, stir it around, bring it out coated in her juices and then whip her steadily, the stings of pain made sharper by the wet leather. But with the pain came a pleasure so immense she could barely contain it. It changed her somehow, gave her a strength she'd never had before.

Uwe was changed, too. It was as though all the fury that had driven him to be cruel, to kill, had dissipated. As their couplings grew more intense, the summary executions ceased altogether. Oh, he was still capable of great cruelty - one day he flogged a man within an inch of his life - but when the cruelty emerged he would later beg her to hurt him, to slap him, bite him, whip him with his own crop, as though he were acknowledging both his wrongdoings and his need for punishment. It was then that Desiree learned that the pleasure of giving could be just as great as receiving.

Much of Uwe's cruelty was replaced with kindness. He looked after Desiree, and by extension looked after her friends as well. He brought extra food, made sure that all the women in Canada had warm clothing, and, best of all, he made sure they all had real leather shoes, not the wooden clogs common in the camp.

While their sexual encounters remained intense, they didn't always meet alone for that reason. There were times when Uwe called her to his office just so he could talk to her, hold her, kiss her, stroke her hair.

"I am a different man," he told her. "You've made me different. And for that I thank you. I don't feel so much hatred anymore; you've brought me peace."

And then he began whispering the words to her, only when in the deepest throes of passion and always in German, never in French, perhaps thinking she wouldn't understand: ich liebe dich. Sometimes he would whisper it over and over until he came, and Desiree could feel a new intensity in his climaxes.

At the same time Uwe seemed deeply troubled, and more and more reluctant to indulge in the violence that had marked their couplings from the very start. Desiree, too, was troubled; by her response to him, by the feelings; she refused to call them love, she had for him. She didn't know how to define them because she couldn't define him.

He was a man. He was also a monster. He was her lover. And he was also a killer. He gave her both pain and pleasure and, more often than not, the two seemingly opposing sensations were inextricably bound together. He was a complex knot of contradictions that she felt she'd never be able to untangle.

Then it had all come abruptly to an end that night when he had brought the violence to a stop. He had disappeared from her life, and, as he had promised her, she was freed, only to find out later that he had died on the Eastern Front.

Desiree sat up straight. She knew now that she had not only loved Uwe, she had loved him deeply. And there was a powerful connection between her love for Uwe and the feelings she had developed for Hans. She thought back to their last encounter in Hans's office. There had been that moment when Hans had held her the way Uwe often had, kissing her cheek, stroking her hair. She had almost succumbed to that familiar tenderness before abruptly pulling away from him.

Desiree realized with a start that the pain in Hans's eyes had mirrored the pain she'd refused to recognize in Uwe's eyes, but now could see as clearly as she could see the light of the day. Uwe had loved her. He had told her again and again that he loved her. And she had never once told him how she felt, because she didn't want to feel anything for him.

Had she told him, it might have brought him some comfort. It might have sustained him, kept him going, kept him alive. But she hadn't told him, and she would have to live with that for the rest of her life.

Desiree resolved then and there that she wouldn't let the same thing happen between her and Hans. She wasn't able to call it love. It frightened her to even think about that; what they shared was quite obviously something more than lust. Knowing that, she couldn't hurt Hans any further. In fact, she never wanted to hurt anyone, ever again.

***

Hans had wept for more than an hour; for himself, for Jürgen, for everything they had and everything they'd lost. He realized now that he did love Jürgen. He hadn't wanted to admit it, to himself or to Jürgen.

But Jürgen, with all his wisdom and sensitivity, had known that Hans loved him. He'd probably known it all along. But Hans hadn't been able to say the words to the one person he loved in this world, and if anything happened to Jürgen, he would have to live with that knowledge for the rest of his life.

And at that moment, Hans, too, came to a resolution; that he would no longer bury his feelings. It was difficult for him; even say the word with regard to himself, but Jürgen was right. He did have feelings and he would never again allow them to go unexpressed. Not when they had the power to change the course of his life, and the lives of the people he cared about; Jürgen, and also Desiree.

Chapter Ten

Now that he was back in Angoulême, Hans found himself once again face to face with his dilemma. The Gruppenführer was getting anxious. He wasn't happy with the fact that Hans had let the matter of the American dollars "slip" through his fingers.

What the Gruppenführer didn't know was that Hans hadn't exactly let the matter slip. He knew exactly where the dollars had gone, what they had purchased, and where the purchased goods had been delivered. He was simply biding his time before moving in, before giving the order for the arrests.

It had all been ridiculously easy, and he hadn't even needed to involve Desiree. He simply followed the logical trail he knew existed once he determined that she indeed held the American dollars. After all, he had tracked her movements steadily for well over a month. It hadn't been difficult at all.

Hans had not spoken with Desiree since that afternoon in his office. He had Hermann call her to verify the menus for his soirée and her arrival time, the tools and help she would need in the kitchen. Everything had been arranged without him, and that was exactly how Hans wanted it. He would have no contact with Desiree until she arrived at his townhouse that Saturday afternoon.

There was a reason for this. There was a reason for all of it.

***

Desiree had been working with Hermann regarding all the plans for Hans' soirée. She had tried calling Hans several times, but he hadn't taken her calls. She imagined he was still hurt by the way she had treated him; she hadn't forgotten the pain in his eyes. But if he refused to speak with her, she had no choice but to wait until she saw him the day of his soirée. At least that was only a day away now.

In the meantime, Desiree had deliveries to make for all the produce she'd picked up. She saw Rene waiting for her outside his restaurant, his usually smiling face dark with concern; his features relaxed once he caught sight of her, but while anxiety was replaced with relief, there was still no smile.

"Thank God you are safe," he said to her when she got out of her truck. She gave him a tight smile in return. Rene turned to his assistant:

"Nicholas, unload our order. You know what it is. I need to speak with Mme. Mendelsohn."

He took Desiree by the arm and steered her into the alley beside the restaurant. When they were at a distance from the street, he turned to her, his face very serious.

"Mon Dieu," he said, as his expression turned to one of surprise, "you don't know, do you?"

"What is it, Rene? Is it Mathieu? Mariette? One of the children?"

"No," he replied. "It's Guy. He's been arrested."

"When?"

"They picked him up this morning. We assume he's being interrogated now, as we speak."

"Anyone else?"

"No."

Desiree drew in a deep breath. "Guy won't talk," she finally said.

"You're probably right. But that doesn't make you any safer. You should leave town, immediately."

"And go where, Rene? Where in occupied France could I hide? How would I survive?"

"They say there are Jews hidden all over."

"They say a great deal, don't they? And I suppose 'they' haven't seen the same trains heading east that we have. Besides, if I were to leave suddenly, wouldn't that make me appear even more suspicious?"

"I could help you...I and others."

"And risk your lives for what?"

"What on earth do you mean? For you, of course."

"Don't even think of it. I'm not worth it, Rene."

She turned as if to walk away, but Rene grabbed her, whirled her back around to face him once more.

"Don't give me that rubbish," he said. "I know you hate yourself, but there are many people who care about you. Stop treating us as though we're nothing to you."

"Perhaps you are nothing to me."

"Oh, stop it. You don't even believe that yourself."

To her great horror, Desiree began to cry. Rene didn't hesitate; he pulled her into his arms and held her close.

"Hush," he whispered. "It's all right."

"I'm sorry," she whispered in reply.

He planted an affectionate kiss on her forehead. "I know you are. Why the devil to you hate yourself so? I'll never understand."

"You don't know what I've done in my life since…my son's death."

It still pained her to mention that horrific event, one that she'd long since learned to bury deep within her. She'd learned not to say his name. He was gone, after all; she could never bring him back, never reverse things as she would have liked, so that he was alive and she was dead. Just to say his name would unleash all that pain and more, and she couldn't bear that. So she tried not to think about him. She had stopped dreaming about him, and she'd forgotten the sound of his voice, but she kept her many photos of him on the walls of her cottage as a constant reminder, to keep the pain from completely slipping away.

Rene laughed. "So, what have you done? Murdered someone? Nothing can be that bad." He rocked her a bit as he held her; the way a father would comfort a weeping child.

"I've hurt people, Rene."

"We all have. What of it?"

"But I've hurt so many…"

He took her face in his hands and looked deep into her tear-filled eyes. His familiar, comforting grin had returned.

"Listen to me," he said. "Are you Hitler?"

Finally, Desiree laughed.

"That's my girl. You see? Believe me, nothing you've done in your lifetime could possibly be any worse."

He pulled a handkerchief from his pocket. "Now dry your tears. We need to talk about what to do to keep you safe."

"There's nothing to be done. I'm sure I would have been arrested by now if I were in any real danger."

"Still, we need to plan ahead. There are ways to get you out of France, through Spain and then Portugal and onto a ship to the Americas. I'll look into it right away."

Desiree looked at him in astonishment.

"What? You weren't expecting someone like me to have such connections?" Rene's response was pained.

"To be honest, no." Desiree didn't mean to hurt him, but it was true.

Rene laughed. "Just a cheerful restaurateur, right? Nice, but not very bright. In other words; harmless."

"That's not fair, Rene."

"It isn't? How do you think of me, then?" The smile was still on his face, the voice still full of good cheer, but there was an edge to it now.

"The way I've always thought of you; as my friend." Desiree reached out then, touched him on the shoulder lightly, not wanting him to read too much into the gesture. Rene placed his hand over hers, patted it gently.

"I know. And for that I'm glad."

Rene knew he couldn't possibly tell Desiree how he really felt about her, as much as he'd like to. But perhaps it was better this way, for both of them. The less invested he was in her personally, the less it would hurt him to be parted from her, and the more he could actually help her. And helping Desiree was what mattered most to him. Perhaps, if there hadn't been a war, things might have been different. But there was a war; with no end to it in sight.

***

Arresting Guy Benneuex had been a wise move, Hans reflected. The Gestapo was interrogating him now. He knew Benneuex was unlikely to talk, but what of it? Let the Gestapo do their job. Hans had never believed in the methods of torture so often employed by that branch of the SS. He knew they weren't effective; that the unique style of understated psychological pressure he had developed over years of detective work was far more potent and devastating.

If Hans really wanted Benneuex to talk, he could have him talking within an hour. At some point he would indeed interrogate Benneuex himself. Right now his priorities lay elsewhere. Something fundamental had changed inside him since that last night with Jürgen. Just thinking of his name brought a sharp twinge of pain, but it was a welcome pain. It was more proof that he could indeed truly feel, that he was alive, that he wasn't simply an automaton.

There had been a letter from Jürgen. The words were veiled to protect them both, since mail was routinely opened throughout the military postal system. But the message was clear:

I think often of the last time we saw each other, of how much we enjoyed each other's company. You are my oldest and dearest friend, and I meant everything I said to you. I want you to know that, although I know how reluctant you are to speak of such matters as friendship, I know you feel the same way.

Hold on to that feeling, and I'll do the same. I expect my work to be quite challenging over the next few months, and I'm not sure when I'll be able to write to you again. I know that you'll write me back, as you always have, but I can't promise that I'll receive it. So if you don't hear from me, don't worry. I'll continue to think of you, as I know you'll continue to think of me.

Let's pray that this war ends soon, and that it won't be as long before we're able to visit again.

With all best wishes,

Your very good friend,

Jürgen

Hans had fought back tears while reading the letter. He had received it at the office, after all, as he did all his mail. In reading it he could hear Jürgen's voice, feel his touch; smell his scent. He took a very deep breath, then neatly folded up the letter. He tucked it carefully inside his wallet, to keep it safe.

Tomorrow was the night of his soirée. He still had not seen or spoken to Desiree. Hermann had made a last call to her today to confirm that she had everything she needed. Now Hans had just one more call to make to put the next step of his plan into action. He took another deep breath, then reached for the telephone.

***

Mathieu helped Desiree bring in the supplies for Guidon's dinner party the next day. He was wishing now that he had never referred that SS Colonel to her. He had heard about the arrest of Guy Benneuex, and he knew that Desiree would be catering the Colonel's soirée tomorrow afternoon, before he and his guests proceeded to dinner here.

Of course Mathieu couldn't be sure that Desiree was working with the Resistance. He had never asked her and never would. He was well aware that it was always better not to know; that simply by knowing he would put not only his own life but also the lives of his wife and children at risk. And he would not endanger his beloved family for anyone; not even Desiree. So rather than ask what he most wanted to know, he asked about her plans for the soirée.

"Do you have everything you need? Are there any pots or utensils you'd like to borrow?"

"No, that won't be necessary," Desiree replied. "I'm fixing a simple selection of hors d'oeuvres. I won't need any special utensils or large pots or pans."

"This colonel...by all accounts, he's a very clever man."

Unable to avoid doing so, Desiree felt herself begin to blush. She tried to keep her face turned away from Mathieu, but he caught her under the chin and turned her to face him.

"Please," he said, looking straight into her eyes, "be very, very careful around this man. Finish the soirée and be done with him."

Desiree felt the hot flush creep across her face. She couldn't hide it; all she could do was to wait for Mathieu's response. He looked at her closely, as though he were analyzing her features, trying to read the truth in them. And then it suddenly dawned on him. He'd seen her blush like this before; she had always blushed whenever he teased her about her lovers.

"Mon Dieu, have you been intimate with this Nazi?"

Desiree tried to turn away from him, but he grabbed her by the shoulders and held her fast.

"Have you gone mad? Do you really have no self-control?"

"It's not like that, Mathieu."

"Then what is it like? Whatever possessed you to get involved with an SS officer?"

Mathieu's grip on her shoulders tightened, and he saw her wince in pain. He let go of her then, and leaned back against the butcher's block in the expansive kitchen.

"I've always worried about you," he said. "I know just how self-destructive you are and always have been. It's something that haunts me and likely always will. Perhaps if things had gone differently between us..."

This time she met his eyes, and her own were fiery and defiant.

"Mathieu, we haven't been lovers for some time. You have no idea what happened to me in the camp."

"I've always wondered."

"I had a lover there."

"I thought as much. Sometimes I think sex is a kind of sustenance to you. It's as though it's something you need to live, that you'd die without it," he said sadly.

"It wasn't like that; well, perhaps at first. But it changed very quickly."

"You fell in love, didn't you?"

Desiree couldn't believe that she had started crying again. Where were all these tears coming from? Why wasn't she able to stop them the way she always had been in the past? She couldn't possibly go on in this way.

"There's nothing wrong with that. I know you've never had that particular feeling for another woman, even though you've slept with them. But it's common for two prisoners to find comfort in each other. It happens between men, as well."

"You don't understand. My lover wasn't a woman."

"So you found a man to love there," Mathieu said. And then his eyes lit with realization. He looked at her thoughtfully.

"You fell in love with a guard," he finally said. "A Nazi."

"Yes," she whispered.

They stood in silence for several minutes while Mathieu pondered this new revelation. Finally, he looked back up and into her eyes again.

"He was kind to you, wasn't he?"

Desiree hesitated, and he looked at her curiously once more. Again, light dawned for him.

"He was kind to you, but he also hurt you."

Desiree cried even harder then: "yes."

"And you enjoyed it."

"Yes."

Again, the two lapsed into silence. Mathieu grabbed a kitchen towel, stepped forward and gently wiped at the tears on Desiree's face, catching them as they cascaded down her cheeks.

He had always wondered if Desiree had pursued her fantasies with another. There were times, when he was making love to her, that she wanted him to be much rougher, to slap and bite her. But Mathieu had never been able to bring himself to do so. Had it been a game of sorts, he might have considered it, but he had always felt that it was much more than a game to her. It seemed to be a form of punishment, and he did not want to be the one to punish her. This wasn't the primary reason for their break up, but it had been an important part of it.

Mathieu didn't tell Desiree to stop, or try to comfort her; he simply let her cry as he carefully mopped up her tears. Somehow he had sensed that this was something she needed to do, and it went on for several minutes before he spoke again.

"Have you had contact with him since then?"

"He's dead now. He was killed on the Eastern Front. But…before he was transferred…he was the one who had me freed."

Mathieu tilted Desiree's chin up once again so he could look deep into her eyes, and she found his steady gaze somehow comforting.

"Listen to me," he said. "Listen very carefully. None of us can ever really predict how we might react in an extreme situation."

He paused for a moment to mop up a few more of her tears.

"All we can really do is learn from our reactions to such situations. You fell in love with a Nazi. He hurt you, but he also saved your life. Perhaps you have feelings for this SS Colonel because of him."

"Yes," she breathed.

"But he's a different person, Desiree. He's not the man you loved, and he never can be. And that's why you must be careful. We still don't know this man's motives."

***

It had been a difficult and unsettling day for Desiree; full of revelations she had never expected to make. She had a long day ahead of her, so she went to bed early that night to get as much rest as possible. She tossed and turned for quite a while before she finally fell asleep.

She dreamed again. Of Uwe, and it was so vivid she could smell his beautiful pink-gold skin, taste the sweetness of his sweat, the flavor of his tongue. He was making love to her; his large, muscular body engulfed her completely, one hand cradling her head, the other gripping her behind, holding her up to meet his thrusts. His golden hair was in disarray, a few locks over his forehead, obscuring his sharp, blue eyes. His long, thick cock was deep inside her, and they were both trembling and moaning with pleasure.

"Bite me," he suddenly breathed, "please, please bite me, bite me…"
She cut him off when she sunk her teeth into first one pec, then the other.

"Gott, ja," he growled as he increased the speed of his thrusts. "More, bitte."

She nipped him all over his chest and up one shoulder to his throat, and sunk her teeth into the tender flesh there. He whimpered, then let her head fall back to the bed, both hands now gripping her behind tightly as he ground himself inside her.

And then it started, the whispering: Ich liebe dich. Ich liebe dich. Ich liebe dich. Ich liebe dich. Ich liebe dich. It seemed to go on and on and on, and then suddenly it stopped, and he was different somehow, he felt different around her and inside her, and she opened her eyes. Hans was above her now, holding her up, his hips were meeting hers, and his beautiful hazel eyes gazed deep into her dark brown ones. There was so much need and desire in those eyes, and something else as well; she couldn't tell what it was, only that it was something she both wanted and didn't want to see there.

"Ich liebe dich," he whispered, his voice silken and sweet, and his eyes never left hers; then he groaned heavily and she could feel him filling her, and she came, too.

And woke up, and began shaking all over. For when she found herself alone in her bed, she was once again awash with a passionate hunger for a man she knew she shouldn't want at all; and yet she did, more than she had ever wanted anyone.

***

Hans had made his move. Tomorrow morning the arrests would be made. It would all be over and done with well in advance of his soirée. His plan had been set into motion.

He would see Desiree again tomorrow. His heart beat like a trip hammer just at the thought of it, and the hunger he'd been repressing over the last two weeks rose up again, powerfully and irrepressibly. But in spite of that desire, or perhaps because of it, it was a reunion he anticipated with far more dread than pleasure.

Chapter Eleven

Desiree was loading her truck with the supplies for Hans's soirée when she spotted someone on a bicycle peddling madly up the dirt road to her cottage. As the figure got closer, she saw who it was; Rene's assistant, Nicholas. He came to a halt just short of her truck.

"Madame," he said, breathless, "I have a message for you, from M. Charlont."

"Rene? Why didn't he telephone?"

"He didn't want to use the telephone, Madame. He said you'd understand when you read the message." He handed her an envelope.

Desiree very quickly tore open the envelope and unfolded the sheet within it.

Desiree,
Several people in the surrounding towns were arrested this morning. All were found to be harboring weapons. Be careful in using your telephone.
Rene

Desiree went pale. Her hand shook as she dug into her pocket to retrieve a couple of francs for the young man.

"Madame, no. That's not necessary."

"Take it," she said firmly, shoving the bills into his hand. Before Nicholas could say another word, Desiree climbed into her truck and sped off.

Her heart pounded as she drove to Hans's townhouse. For a moment she thought of driving on, of letting the truck take her out of town and as far as she could go. But she knew that running away without any plan wouldn't work. It would raise suspicions instead.

Desiree pulled over to the side of the road and sat back, trying to catch her breath. She had to think.

The only explanation for the arrests was that Guy had talked. But that didn't explain why she hadn't been arrested, and that didn't necessarily mean that Hans had anything to do with it.

Desiree leaned forward, her arms on the steering wheel. Hans had to be involved. Why else would he be in a relatively small town like Angoulême? He might not arrest her that very night, but it was bound to happen. His methods were just different with her. She was surely as much his prey as Guy had been, but perhaps she was the prey he preferred to toy with.

Desiree started her truck once more. She would face Hans head on, if it came to that. Perhaps it would happen when she arrived at the townhouse, or perhaps it would happen after the soirée. Whatever the case, she was ready to confront him.

Hermann was waiting for her when she arrived at the townhouse, and he helped her carry in the supplies. Faber's cook housekeeper had everything ready to help her prepare the hors d'oeuvres. Severine was a kindly older woman with a worn but good-humored face, a grey bun and soft grey eyes that had obviously seen a great deal of life.

"Is there anything else you need, ladies? If not, I'll return to my boarding house to change," said Hermann.

"I believe we have everything," Desiree said. "Where are the wines and the champagne?"

"The whites and the champagne are chilling," Severine answered, opening the icebox to show her. "I've set up a few reds to be opened and aired in advance."

"And where is the Colonel?" Desiree kept her voice nonchalant in asking.

"He's upstairs dressing, Madame," Hermann told her. "I'll be off then, if you don't need me for anything more."

"Yes, be off with you! Let us get to work," Severine told him, shooing him away with great flourish and a broad grin that he returned in equal measure. It was obvious the two had known each other for a while and were fond of each other.

Desiree found she liked Severine a great deal. The woman was a good fifteen years older than her, but treated Desiree with respect, deferring to all her requests and directions. As the two worked side by side, she quickly learned that Severine was not only very good in the kitchen, she was also great company.

"How long have you worked for the Colonel?" Desiree asked.

"Mon Dieu, it seems like forever, but in reality it's only been a year."

Desiree laughed. "What makes it seem like forever?"

"He's a curious man," Severine began, her tone more serious. "Sometimes he can be very thoughtful, but at other times; well, not so thoughtful."

"In what way?"

"He'll shout a bit, or perhaps ignore you completely if he's displeased with something you've done. There are times when he is very morose, and times when he's utterly charming. He's a very mercurial man. It's difficult to know what to expect from him."

"Do you like working for him?" Desiree continued.

Severine thought about that for a few minutes. "It's curious," she said finally, "but I never really thought about that until you asked. Work is work, after all, and if the pay is good, who cares? But now that I think of it, yes, I do like working for him. He is a Nazi, of course, and his bite is indeed as bad as his bark, but..."

"But?"

"But for some odd reason that I can't quite fathom, I like him."

"He seems very likeable..." Desiree began cautiously.

"Oh, yes. As I said, he can be quite charming, but that's not why I like him." Severine paused to look at Desiree, her grey eyes twinkling.

"Why, then?"

"Because, as hard as he tries to hide it; and that's very hard indeed, inside he's as soft and pliable as fresh caramel." Severine smiled at the thought.

"You seem to know a lot about him," Desiree said.

"Not really. I just know a lot about people, or at least I think I do. I should hope so, at my age!"

Both women laughed, and went on chatting cheerfully as they continued working together.

***

The food had been prepared, the first trays filled, and they were finally ready for the soirée. Desiree had changed her blouse and put on a fresh apron, and Severine had changed her dress and her apron. The waiters were there, ready to serve the wine and carry the trays.

Desiree's heart fluttered when Hans at last entered the kitchen; immaculately groomed and in his best dress uniform, with all his medals on display. She couldn't help but smile, remembering the night they had met.

Hans smiled right back at Desiree as though nothing had happened, but his heart pounded just at the sight of her.

"It is wonderful to see you again," he told her. "I have so looked forward to this evening, to see all that you've prepared for me and my guests."

Desiree and Severine stepped aside to let him examine the carefully prepared trays. Hans stepped forward and bent down to examine the hors d'oeuvres more closely.

"Excellent. Everything looks superb. Severine, would you excuse us, please? I'd like a moment alone with Madame Mendelsohn."

"Certainement, Monsieur Colonel."

Once Severine had left the kitchen, Hans straightened up and moved closer to Desiree. He hesitated for a moment, then brought a hand up to her face. His fingers felt smooth and warm against her cheek. Desiree wanted so much to lean into that hand, but she resisted the urge to do so.

"You left so quickly the other day," he said softly.

"I know, and I'm sorry for that."

"I didn't want you to leave. I wanted to hold you. We had just made love, after all…"

She looked him in the eye. "Had we?"

Hans was puzzled and there was another quick flash of pain in his eyes at her remark. Then he smirked and removed his hand from her cheek.

"Well, I had made love, at least," he said, his voice bitter.

"We had sex," she told him, and the words sounded too harsh even to her. "It was very good sex-"

"Very good sex," he interrupted with a grin and a twinkle in his eye.

"But it was just sex." Desiree winced inside at the words. And she had told herself she never wanted to hurt anyone again! She wished she could take the words back, but she froze instead.

The grin had nearly vanished; just a touch of it remained, and that touch was tinged with irony. Hans gazed at her intently for quite a while, and Desiree began to feel very uncomfortable under his relentless stare.

They heard the bell ring in the distance, and Severine's voice as she opened the door to greet the first guest.

"We'll discuss this later," Hans told her. "My guests are arriving now."

"Hans…" Desiree didn't want him to leave with so much unsaid. "Later."

He left, and she heard him warmly welcome the first arrivals. The doorbell continued to ring, and Desiree left the kitchen to help Severine, quickly taking on the task of gathering coats and caps.

There was a steady flow of guests for a good half hour. Desiree dashed into the kitchen to check on the status of the trays. A few empty ones had already returned, ready to be refilled. She dashed back to let Severine know that she'd have to stay in the kitchen. Another guest had just arrived, and she quickly took his coat and cap.

The doorbell rang again just as she was hanging up the coat, and Desiree heard a curiously familiar voice. She turned, ready to take the man's coat and cap, and found herself face to face with the young Gestapo officer she'd met at the tavern.

His sharp blue eyes registered surprise for a fraction of a second, and then settled into their familiar, sardonic gaze. Desiree unsuccessfully fought the blush that bloomed in her cheeks. He didn't say anything, simply removed his long, black leather coat and handed it to her with his cap. Then, with a slight smirk on his face, he strode into the main parlor.

"You know him?" Severine asked, curious.

"Just in passing…I've got to get back to the kitchen to fill the trays. They're coming back quickly, now."

"Ah, that's a good sign. They must be enjoying the food. You run along, then. There shouldn't be many more guests."

For the next half hour, Desiree was quite busy preparing for and refilling the trays, which came back in rapid succession. It wasn't long before Severine was able to join her, and, after another busy half hour, things finally began to slow down enough for them each to take a quick break.

There were stairs leading down to a small garden just off the kitchen, so Desiree decided to have a cigarette. She welcomed the cool breeze that greeted her when she opened the door. She went out onto the small, covered landing, settled back against the railing and lit a cigarette while she pondered her latest interaction with Hans. She had almost finished when she heard a rustle in the kitchen.

"Severine?" She asked.

"No."

It was the young Major. Desiree stubbed out her cigarette and went back inside. There he stood, wine glass in hand, that sardonic grin on his face.

"We meet again," he said. "Imagine my surprise."

"Why should it be a surprise?"

"I don't know; perhaps because I didn't picture you as a chef."

"Well, you were right in a way," Desiree responded. "I'm not a chef per se, I'm a caterer."

"Is that all you are?"

Desiree's heart nearly stopped, but she didn't hesitate to answer. "Yes."

The Major's eyes searched hers for quite a while, but she managed to convey a calm façade, although it felt like her heart was hammering in her chest. He was as striking as she remembered, with that pale skin and thin, red mouth, and the image of that beautiful face in the throes of passion once again filled her mind.

His eyes softened. "I'll be honest. I was hoping you would come back. Otherwise I was going to try to find you."

Desiree froze, and again the two stood in silence, staring each other down. Then Desiree saw the sadness creep back into those icy blue eyes, and the smile that came with it was equally sad; and familiar as well.

Then she remembered. It was the same smile he wore when she was dressing to leave, and the last thing she saw before she closed the door behind her. How had she missed the sadness in that smile?

"I'm glad I saw you again tonight," he said finally. "Otherwise I might have continued to entertain the notion that I could somehow become involved with you. Now I know it won't happen. So I don't have to think about you anymore."

Desiree reached out to him. "Major…"

He drew away quickly. "Don't. Don't do that. Don't pity me."

Desiree pulled back her hand.

"There's nothing to pity, after all," he said. "I told you before; I'm used to it."

He smiled again and was about to leave, when he stopped suddenly, clicked his heels and bowed to her.

"Madame," he said, then rose up, turned and left the kitchen.

Desiree took several deep breaths. She tried hard not to think about it, but she couldn't escape the fact that she had hurt this young man, and she had also hurt Hans, yet again. What was it in her that wanted to hurt them?

Was it because they were Nazis? But Uwe had been a Nazi, and she had loved him. Yet she'd also hated herself for loving him. So why had she felt so drawn to Hans and the young Major? And why did what she felt for Hans in particular seem so powerful and so frightening? Desiree thought hard.

The uniforms.

She had always loved uniforms because they reminded her of her long dead father, and how handsome he had looked in his uniform in the last war. But that was too simple and obvious an answer to what she was sure brought forth a deeper, more primal feeling.

Desiree remembered the intensity of her first encounter with Uwe, the feel and smell of the rough wool of his tunic against her back when he took her. The strange comfort she'd felt when he'd held her close afterwards. Then she remembered those times when he'd cuddled her in his office, how she'd buried her face in his shoulder, rubbing her cheeks against that same rough wool. And she remembered those times when she had knelt before him, opened his trousers, and gazed up at him in all his uniformed splendor as she took him in her mouth, how she clung to those wool trousers when he came and she swallowed his seed.

It had been the same with Hans. She had been mesmerized by her first sight of him in his dress uniform. She couldn't help smiling tonight when she saw him in it again. And that day in his office, she had buried her face in the rough wool of his uniformed shoulder, even bit down on it hard when she came.

And she had been almost thunderstruck by the Major's beautiful black uniform. She couldn't remember anyone else in the bar. She heard voices when she tried to remember and realized it had been crowded with people, but she could not remember a single face, not even the bartender, and she had spoken to him as well. She had been so spellbound by the young Major that she literally couldn't see anyone else. And when he had pulled her into the alley to kiss her, she was thrilled and nearly lost herself in that kiss.

Suddenly it came to her. She had been mourning Uwe; mourning him and missing him terribly and not wanting to admit it. And it was almost as though she were taking him back inside her when she was with Hans and the young Major.

But that wasn't the whole story, either. After all, she'd met plenty of soldiers since the war began and hadn't thought of them as anything other than soldiers. She'd enjoyed seeing all the uniforms, but she hadn't fallen in love with any of them. Uwe was the first one she had fallen in love with and her relationship with him had been very, very different from every other relationship she'd had with a man, or woman, for that matter.

There was the jumble of emotions she felt with him, everything from severe pain and abject terror to intense arousal and the thrill of the forbidden. She had felt much of the same with both Hans and the young Major.

The Major was simply a ship that passed in the night. However harsh that might sound, it was the truth. Now she regretted the pain she'd brought him.

But there was much, much more at work in her relationship with Hans. It was that odd sense of familiarity, of a shared outlook of the world, almost of a shared soul. And what all that added up to was the very real possibility - as terrifying as it was to think about - of actually falling in love again; of loving another human being again and, of course, of facing the possibility of suffering yet another loss. She wasn't sure if she could survive another one. There had been far too many losses in her life.

But there was no turning back now. Desiree knew what she needed to do, and she would do it.

***

The guests were leaving, and Hans would soon go with them. Desiree didn't want him to leave without having a chance to speak with him. She caught up with him and Hermann as they were putting on their coats.

"Hans…I need to speak with you," she began cautiously.

He hesitated for a moment, looking straight into her eyes. He saw a plea there; an entreaty, and he somehow felt he couldn't turn away from it.

"Hermann, I'll meet you outside the front door once you've brought the car round. Just honk the horn for me."

"Jawohl, Standartenführer."

Hans turned back to Desiree as soon as Hermann had left; his eyes full of concern."

"What is it, Desiree?"

"It wasn't true…what I said before. I didn't mean it."

He brought a hand up to her cheek again. "I know," he told her.

"I wanted to hurt you," it was hard for her to say it.

"I know you did. I wanted to hurt you, too, but I don't want to anymore."

"I don't either." Her voice was firm.

He stroked her cheek lightly. As much as he wanted to kiss her, this wasn't the right moment for either of them.

"Help Severine clean up," he said. "Then will you wait for me here? I want to talk with you some more."

"Yes," Desiree breathed. She lifted her mouth to his, awaited his kiss. She was so warm, so open to him and her scent was driving him mad. It took everything Hans had to keep from kissing her. He smiled at her and stroked her cheek once more, then turned away.

"Severine!" he called.

Severine came out of the kitchen, drying her hands quickly on her apron.

"Yes, Monsieur Colonel?"

"Desiree will help you with the washing up. Then she's to remain here, to wait for my return. Please show her to the library when you're done. Then you're welcome to retire for the night whenever you wish."

He paused for a moment, then smiled warmly at Severine.

"You've done a wonderful job for me today," he told her. "Thank you." The car horn sounded outside.

"I must leave now," he went on. "I'll be back as quickly as I can. Again, thank you for all you've done today, Severine. I'll be seeing you later, Desiree." He disappeared out the front door, and they heard his footsteps as he hurried down the marble stairs.

Severine was astonished. "He's never thanked me before," she told Desiree. "He'll tell me I've done a good job, or praise my cooking, but that's the first time he's ever actually thanked me."

She turned to look at Desiree. "He's fond of you, I think. Are you fond of him?"

Desiree hesitated for a moment. "Yes," she finally said, "I am."

She hadn't wanted to admit this to herself, but as soon as she said the words to Severine she knew they were true, and somehow, a huge weight had been lifted from her shoulders.

Chapter Twelve

"Sex is a powerful truth—perhaps the most powerful and ruthless truth of all. Because people's passions don't lie. Oh, they can be covered—hidden for an entire lifetime. But they don't lie. And if we dare to admit our passions, give them life, then they have the power to destroy every hypocrisy and mendacity in their path."
Richard C. Zimler

It was close to ten when Hermann finally brought Hans home, and he wondered if Desiree was still waiting for him. He hoped she was. He needed very much to talk to her. He had to tell her the truth. She might hate him for it, but he had to do it.

Hans opened the double doors to the library carefully, not wanting to startle her. He needn't have worried; Desiree lay fast asleep on one of the two facing sofas, a blanket pulled around her.

He approached her as quietly as possible. She looked so small and so innocent as she slept, almost like a child. Hans wondered what she had been like as a little girl, and then he remembered that she hadn't had much of a childhood, just a few blissful years before both her parents were taken from her during the flu epidemic. Her life had then become a succession of boarding schools just like his.

It was one of the things they shared in common: a lost childhood, an early end to innocence and beauty. Desiree was a little more fortunate in that she had the memory of parents who had loved and cared for her. Hans didn't lose his parents early - both had lived to a ripe old age - but he had never had their love. It was one of the aspects of his life that had so hardened him, and even now when he thought of it, he experienced the same mixture of pain and rage that he'd suffered from for as long as he could remember.

It wasn't until he met Jürgen that Hans had finally felt the love of another human being. For years he had held a reserve of guilt for that forbidden love and for the intense need that drove him to seek men as well as women. He had been ashamed of it, though never ashamed of Jürgen, whom he now knew he would always love. He couldn't imagine not loving Jürgen. It was Jürgen who had taught him how to love; no, they had taught each other. They had both been lonely and abandoned, and they'd found a lasting solace in each other. There was no shame in that; it was something to treasure.

As he gazed down at Desiree, Hans felt all the guilt and shame melt away. He could love Jürgen freely now. And if he was capable of loving Jürgen, he might also be able to love Desiree; although the thought terrified him as much as it thrilled him.

He knelt down by the sofa, reached out and gently shook her shoulder. "Wake up, Desiree," he said softly.

She opened her eyes and looked at him, all sleep-soft and vulnerable. He very nearly felt his heart give way at those large, dark eyes of hers, so beautifully framed by long, black eyelashes. At that moment she was achingly lovely, and he couldn't resist; he leaned over and gave her a gentle kiss on the lips.

She returned his kiss just as gently, and they went on kissing for several minutes, slowly, savoring how their lips met and caressed. They each opened their mouths and darted the very tips of their tongues together lightly, again and again, a touch so soft and so tender it was almost unbearable; until neither could stand it any longer and they let their mouths and tongues fully meet. Hans couldn't remember ever having experienced a kiss so sweet.

Desiree sat up. Hans shifted on his knees until he was between her legs, and they embraced each other and kissed deeply, with a growing urgency. Desiree wrapped her legs around Hans's waist and clung to him as their kisses grew hungrier, needier, and all they could hear was the rhythm of their breathing as it grew harsher, the soft press of their lips meeting, the low murmurs and sighs they shared.

There was nothing Hans wanted more than to continue that kiss, to see where their passion took them, but he had to speak to her. He could put it off no longer. He slowly drew away, bringing her forehead down to touch his.

"We must speak," he told her, more firmly this time. He let go of her, rose up and sat down on the sofa opposite, so he could face her.

"I know what you've been doing," Hans began. "I was sent here to get information from you, and to do so by seducing you."

"But it didn't turn out that way," he went on quickly. "I wouldn't let it. I found other ways to get the information I needed. I didn't have to get it from you. I found it myself, without having to compromise you."

Desiree was thunderstruck. She had been right. She had been his prey. But although her suspicions were now confirmed, she didn't fear him. Perhaps she recognized that something larger was at stake between them, because she now knew, almost instinctively, when she had stopped being his prey and become something else to him.

"You've heard about the arrests" he went on.

"Yes," Desiree said softly. "What will happen to them?"

"I'm doing what I can to see that they're sent to camps rather than shot. That's the best I can do, and I can't promise that I'll succeed." There was little he could do, after all, when it came to the will of the Gestapo.

"You knew about me all along."

"Yes. I knew when you had the American dollars, and I knew who received them from you, and when. I knew what was purchased with them, when you received the goods, and when and to whom you delivered them."

"How?" Desiree was thunderstruck.

"I can't tell you that. I'm sure you realize why."

"And yet you haven't arrested me…why?" She had to know, somehow it was crucial that she know.

"Because I had to save you. I had to save your life."

Just like Uwe.

Hans was saving her life. Just as Uwe had. I will free you, Uwe had said, and in doing so he'd saved her life. Now Hans was doing the same: I had to save your life.

She looked into his beautiful, ever-changing eyes, and they had once again become that deep emerald green she loved most. And in that moment when she gazed into these eyes so green, she knew that there was indeed something bigger between them. She still didn't want to name it; she was too afraid, but she knew it was powerful, and strong, and she didn't want to wait any longer to express it.

Hans knew it, too, and he wasn't able to wait any longer, either. He had been looking deeply into Desiree's rich, dark eyes. Now he rose up from his sofa, walked over to her, and reached out a hand.

Desiree took that hand, rose up and stood close to him. Hans gazed at her almost reverently, his eyes shining with a new light. He stroked her cheek, her hair; with one finger traced her ear, then let that same finger draw a path down to the base of her throat.

It was quiet in the library; so very, very quiet. All that could be heard was their deep, measured breathing and the soft ticking of the clock on the fireplace mantel.

"Come with me," Hans said, taking hold of Desiree's hand, cradling her arm in his. They were halfway up the staircase and had just reached the first landing when Hans suddenly pulled her to him, pushed her up against the wall and kissed her fiercely, passionately, his mouth hungrier and more insistent that it had ever been before. Desiree wrapped her arms around his neck and returned that kiss with equal fervor, one hand sneaking up into his silky hair.

Hans pulled away, breathing hard. "I could take you right here," he whispered, and he nipped at her earlobe and her throat as he pressed his arousal against her. "I want you so much."

"And I want you -"

Hans cut her off with another fervent kiss, and when he pulled away again he leaned into her, touched his forehead to hers once more.

"We'll have each other," he told her softly, "but in my bed. I want to see all of you, touch all of you."

Hans led her up the rest of the stairs and into his bedroom, where he pulled her into another passionate embrace. Now, at last, he could lose himself in her, let himself be carried away by his passion, and he felt Desiree meet that passion in a collision of mouths and tongues and bodies that lifted them both ever closer to bliss.

Hans fell to his knees before her, lifted her skirt and pulled down her underwear, then buried his mouth between her legs. He licked and kissed her there; she was already very wet for him, and the scent and taste of her nearly drove him wild. He couldn't get enough of her, and he teased and tempted her with his tongue until at last she pulled him up, and they worked furiously to undress each other.

Desiree gazed at Hans with great pleasure when he was at last naked. His body was beautiful; lean, compact, mature in a way that only made him more masculine. It was a man's body, not a boy's; a body that she could see had experienced much in life.

His erect cock rose proudly from a nest of soft, brown curls; the moist, pink head peeking cheekily out of its darker foreskin. She had seen this cock, tasted it, felt it inside her, but now it was as though she was seeing it for the very first time.

Hans shivered under her appreciative gaze, and the warm, sweet smile that came with it filled him with a brand new pleasure. Men had looked at him like this, but Desiree was the first woman he had ever met who was unafraid to gaze frankly at his body, to truly admire it.

Over the years Desiree had learned the contours and rhythms of a man's body, how to tease it and please it, and she was anxious to explore this one. She took Hans by complete surprise when she pushed him back onto the bed and climbed over him. She was eager to explore every inch of him. His scent - a musky mixture of sweat, soap and tobacco - was almost intoxicating.

Hans gazed up at her in wonder, pulled her down for a kiss, but she wouldn't let him roll her over and under him. It was her turn to smell and touch and taste him.

Desiree kissed him all over his face and his throat while her hands wandered around his body, exulting in the softer, more pliable feel of his flesh. As she'd grown older and the men she'd known had grown older with her, Desiree had learned to revel in the wondrous texture of an older man's skin. Not as tight and smooth as a younger man's, but infinitely more pleasing to the touch, with all the imperfections that a life well-lived had to offer. It was like the difference between a wine of recent vintage and one that had been allowed to age and mellow until its color and flavor were enriched and enlivened. Hans's body was all of that and more.

Hans relaxed and let himself enjoy every touch of her hands, every press of her lips against his flesh. Not since Frau Wennig, all those years ago when he was just sixteen - had it really been more than thirty - had a woman so thoroughly explored his body, and his breath quickened with each caress. He trembled when Desiree buried her nose in the soft, fine hair under one arm, then licked him there; and when she kissed her way across to the other side to do the same, stopping briefly to nibble lightly on his collar bone, he gasped.

Desiree stroked the light dusting of hair on his chest, pinched his nipples - so tiny and yet so taut - and when she bent down to kiss, lick, suck and bite them, Hans let out a low moan so raw and so feral that it set her on fire.

His hands were now roaming all over her body, caressing every inch within reach. Her damp cleft was pressed against one thigh, and he flexed the muscle there almost imperceptibly, which only stimulated her further, and then Desiree, too, moaned in pleasure.

She grew even wetter and Hans ached to taste her again and was sorely tempted to roll her off and under him so he could do just that. But the aching need to have her continue her exquisite exploration of his body overruled that desire, so Hans bit his lip and held on for dear life, keeping his lust at bay.

Desiree kissed her way down his chest, swirled her tongue in his navel, and traced the fine trail of hair that ran down his belly to the nest of hair that surrounded his erection. She rubbed her nose and mouth in that luxuriant forest of curls and breathed in deeply, inhaling the rich and distinctive scent of male musk and sweat.

Hans groaned and opened his eyes to watch when he felt her tongue slide up his erection, then lightly tease the head. But he nearly cried out when her mouth engulfed him and she began sliding slowly down and back up again.

"Stop," he cried out, his voice desperate. "I can't hold on much longer."

Desiree planted a light kiss on the very tip of his cock, then crawled back up his body to meet his fiery gaze. Those emerald green eyes shone brightly now, and Hans gathered Desiree back in his arms, held her close and kissed her once more.

"You beautiful, bewitching creature," he breathed, "it's my turn now."

He had been aching to touch and kiss her soft, full breasts, and he was at last able to roll her on her back to do so. He lightly caressed her breasts, darting out his tongue to playfully tease her nipples before engulfing each one within his mouth and lightly suckling on it.

It was such bliss to be able to at last truly enjoy her bare flesh. The taste of her skin was as sweet as the taste of her sex, and she was just as lushly soft all over as Hans had imagined. His mind reeled at all that he wanted to do to her. He wanted to bury his face in her breasts. He wanted to lick her again. He wanted to be inside her. The need to taste her once more won out, bolstered by the desire to feel her thighs wrapped around his head.

Hans rose up, lifted Desiree by the hips and roughly brought her up to his mouth until she was nearly on her head. He pushed his tongue inside her, and the move was so primitively possessive that Desiree gasped, then choked out a groan as his tongue withdrew to swirl through all that sweet cream.

His tongue moved down even lower, to that most often untouched part of her, and licked and swirled there as well. Desiree cried out when she felt the tip of that tongue lightly penetrate her, and Hans let loose with a growl so animalistic that it touched something primitive in her, made her growl in response.

His urgency was increasing and, still growling, Hans roughly licked his way back up again. He had never felt so raw with a woman. He'd been like this with men, but to experience that wild, primitive part of him with a woman was thrilling. Hans took her tender bud in his mouth and swirled his tongue around it, then sucked it hard until she came with another sharp cry.

It was only then that he lowered her back down on the bed. "I need to be inside you," he said, his voice thick, his breath heavy. "Do you want my cock inside you?"

"Yes," she breathed. "Please. Now."

He pulled her legs up until her ankles were around his neck, then thrust deep inside her. They both groaned at that initial penetration, and then Hans began to fuck her, grunting with each rough, deep thrust, and Desiree matched his grunts as she lifted her hips to meet them.

It was raw and wild and exciting beyond belief, and when Desiree opened her eyes she saw Hans gazing down at her in wonder, his eyes now amber and ablaze with fire. She was going to come again, but then he pulled out suddenly, lowered her legs to the bed and bent over to kiss her.

"Not yet," Hans whispered softly, "not yet."

"Please…"

"No, not yet."

He rolled Desiree over, shoved a pillow beneath her belly, parted her legs and knelt between them, slowly penetrating her once more. This time Hans moved gently, teasingly, reveling in how hot and wet and tight she was, and how very, very good she felt around his cock.

Awash with sensation, he lay down along the length of Desiree's body, still gripping her hips, thrusting with a smooth, sure rhythm. He nipped at the back of her neck, at her shoulders, felt her shudder and moan. Hans knew he had hit that center of pleasure inside her; he could feel her tremble every time he touched it with his cock, and then Desiree broke into a passionate litany that only further fueled his lust.

"Yes," she cried, "Oh, yes. Right there, yes. Please, please, I need it…"

"Not yet," he breathed into her ear, "not yet."

Desiree could hear the tremor in his voice, knew that he was torturing himself as much as he was torturing her, and she thought she might weep in frustration. And yet it was so sweetly, unbearably pleasurable, the sure and steady press of his cock inside her, right against that exquisite spot. She was close, and she could feel that Hans was close, too, felt his cock swell inside her. She tried to move her hips back, but he held them fast - and then he stopped once more.

"Please," she whimpered, "don't stop."

"Hush," he whispered, "hush now."

Hans held himself very, very still inside her, and Desiree held still as well, and together they listened to the matched thumping of their hearts, the shallow rhythm of their breathing. Hans kissed the back of her neck, slid his tongue along her ear. Gott im Himmel, if he could just lie like this with her forever; the pleasure was so intense, so exquisitely good, he never, ever wanted it to end.

But the urge for release spurred him forward, and he slowly withdrew from her once more. Desiree whimpered again when she felt him slip outside of her body, and he gently, tenderly rolled her onto her back again.

Looking deep into her rich, dark eyes, Hans lifted Desiree's legs over his hips, and she wrapped them around his torso. Then slowly, very, very slowly, he slid back inside her once more. He held very still within her and kissed her deeply, passionately. There was something more in that kiss as well, and Desiree felt it, too, and she returned it with equal fervor.

Then Hans began to move again, and Desiree followed. This time they moved together, matched their rhythms, sharing their pleasure and feeding it to each other.

"Don't stop," Desiree breathed, "please don't stop."

He kissed her again. "I won't this time, I promise," he told her, his voice husky, yet tender and soothing. "I need it as much as you."

Together they increased their thrusts, and Desiree could feel it building inside her; that glorious, inexorable, fevered climb to release, until it burst inside her; the sheer joy of it washing over her, and this time her cry was long and drawn-out, an almost feral howl.

When Hans felt that wave of bliss wash over her, he moved harder, faster. His flesh felt alive with liquid fire and the aching need for completion was so desperate, so acute, and it grew larger, engulfing all his senses, until a lightning bolt shot up and down his spine before bursting free from his body in a series of sharp throbs; and he let loose with a long, loud, growling groan that seemed to reverberate throughout the entire townhouse.

Even Severine, back in the kitchen for a late night glass of milk, heard it. She smiled, and made a note to herself to prepare breakfast for two tomorrow.

Chapter Thirteen

It was still dark outside when Hans awoke, and the light patter of rain against the window was somehow soothing and peaceful. He was pressed up against Desiree from behind, his body molded to hers.

Gott, she was so soft, so very soft. He drew his hand slowly up her thigh to her hip. He was hard again, and he wanted her so much. He didn't want to wake her, but he couldn't help himself, and his caresses became more purposeful.

Hans kissed the back of Desiree's neck, moved a hand over her body and between her legs. She was still damp down there, and when he moved his fingers in and around her flesh he caught the rich scent of their sex: the mingled sweat, her juices, his semen. It was almost intoxicating. His breath grew heavier, his kisses more fervent.

He felt Desiree awaken, knew she was holding still to enjoy his caresses, and then she began to move back against him, pressing the soft, luscious flesh of her heart shaped bottom against his groin, urging him on, which only triggered his lust further. He lifted her leg, pulled it up over his hip and thrust deep inside her. They both heaved a sigh at that initial penetration, as much in relief as in pleasure.

It felt so good, so right to be joined with her again; to be so close to her. Hans could hear her breathing, feel her heartbeat and reveled in the press of her flesh against his. When he closed his eyes he felt he was all sensation, locked together with her in some incredible carnal bliss. And somehow it was all new to him; he who had been with so many women and men, who had done almost everything imaginable sexually. How amazing it was to discover that, after all these years, there were still things to be learned and experienced.

Hans bit his lip, struggled to hold himself still, but Desiree pressed back harder against him, trying to take him deeper inside her while creating the friction they both craved. Hans's kisses grew more fevered as he began to move inside her, and he listened closely as her breath grew increasingly labored. He felt as though he could never get deep enough inside her, and he wanted to so desperately. The drive, the very need to do so was an almost primal urge, as if by doing so their very souls would touch and they'd both know ecstasy.

Desiree seemed to almost instinctively understand and feel that same need; and she reached back behind them both to grab Hans's hip and pull him into her even deeper, while pressing back against him as hard as she could. She moaned then, and Hans whimpered pressing forward as far as he could go, thrusting deeply inside her, nipping passionately at her throat.

Desiree stiffened against Hans and let loose with a soft groan. When he felt the gentle and rhythmic gripping of her sex around him, he drove as deep as he could go and unleashed a heavy groan as his cock throbbed and spurted inside her.

***

It was dawn when Hans awoke once more. The rain had stopped, and he could hear a mourning dove in the distance. Desiree was still asleep, but she had turned over and was facing him now, so he took the opportunity to fully admire her in the tranquility of that early morning.

She was not a thin woman; her curves were lush and full and incredibly soft and welcoming. He was sure some men would consider her too heavy, but Hans had never liked thin, bony women. If he wanted a slender body, he could have that in a man any time. No, he liked his women as womanly as possible: full hips, large breasts and a plush, round bottom were perfect to him. Desiree had all these qualities, and she was as wild and wanton in bed as any man he'd ever had.

His gaze fell on one of the silvery stretch marks on her belly, the lasting marks of having given birth. He had never had children, never even considered doing so, much less considered marriage. He had always been too buried in his work. And there had always been his lust for men to consider. What woman would have a man who so deeply desired other men? But then he'd never considered what it would be like to have a woman love you so much that she would carry your child.

Hans wondered what Desiree had looked like when her belly was rounded with her son. Had he met her twenty years earlier, that child might have been his, and perhaps his life would be very, very different.

Hans smiled and shook his head. What ridiculous thoughts he was having; stupid, foolish thoughts. What kind of father could he have possibly been? It wasn't as though he'd had any real example to follow in his own distant, dismissive father, and there was so much rage and pain inside him he could never have set a positive example for a child. No, there was too much that was twisted and damaged inside him to ever have been a good father.

Desiree shifted a bit in her sleep, which pulled Hans out of his reverie. Gott, how lovely she looked. It was foolish, he knew, but somehow he felt less damaged with her. But he was still not whole, and probably never would be. He didn't believe it was at all possible for someone like him to feel whole. The closest he'd come to feeling so were those blissful months at university when he and Jürgen had first become lovers. That was the first time in his life that Hans had truly felt loved and wanted, and it had given him that little vestige of hope that had carried him throughout his life; that one morsel of humanity that gave him a reason to live.

Somehow Desiree had managed to touch that tiny sliver of life inside him, and he needed that, so that must mean he needed her; and again, that mixture of thrill and fear at the thought filled him completely, and he wanted to drive it away. But at the same time he didn't want to lose it; it was better to feel this turmoil, to experience it, than to return to the emptiness he'd felt for so long. It was better to be human and not an automaton.

Hans reached out then, and drew his finger down one of the shiny, silvery stretch marks on her belly. She woke up then, looked at him and smiled. He smiled back at her, and the hunger rose up in him again. He moved over to her, replaced his finger with his tongue, tracing each of her stretch marks, following them down her belly and to her sex, where the scent of their mingled flavors nearly made him drunk.

He had to taste the two of them together, and when he did he moaned because the mixture was rich and sweet and creamy beyond belief, and he licked and licked and licked at her, gathering as much of that sweetness on his tongue as possible.

Desiree was as excited by his soft sighs and the snuffling sounds of pleasure he made as she was by the touch of his tongue. He was so tender with her and yet so ardent. The way he seemed to savor every touch, every taste, every kiss filled her with incredible joy. When his tongue grazed her swollen bud she moaned and grabbed him by the hair and pulled him closer, and he dove right in with a rough growl.

Hans suckled hungrily on that soft bud, grasping her thighs and pulling her closer to him, bringing her thighs around his neck, luxuriating in the feel of that soft flesh against his face.

He was beginning to learn her body and its subtle signals. He could feel her tense up, knew she was close, felt her tremble when his tongue pressed along one side of her tender clitoris, and he kept it pressed there while he lightly sipped at the tip with his lips. She tensed even more. He continued his caresses with lips and tongue, and she raised her hips to his mouth until she finally stiffened against him and came with a low moan. He withdrew to slide his tongue inside her so he could feel her contractions. To know he'd done this to her, given her such pleasure, made him feel feral and possessive and drove his desire even deeper.

And then Hans couldn't help himself any longer, he had to be inside her again, needed so desperately to be that close to her. He crawled quickly up her body and pulled her hips to his, and slid inside her once more. Every inch of his skin was aflame with desire, desire for her, to be close to her, to feel every aspect of him joined with her, body and soul. The pleasure was fierce and intoxicating, and he trembled with it, burned with it, so aching and desperate to experience that ultimate closeness with this woman, his lover, his mistress, his everything; and oh Gott, she was coming again, gripping him so tightly inside, bringing him closer, closer, closer yet, and then he drove deep inside, as deep as he could go, and came with a throaty roar of pleasure.

Afterwards he held her close, buried his face in her shoulder; enjoyed the feel of his satiated flesh pressed to hers. He felt his cock soften; then slither out of her in a pool of warmth. He rolled off her. At first he was a bit afraid to look at her again, afraid that doing so would rekindle his passion. But after a while, a very short while, he couldn't resist, and when he turned to look at her he was greeted with a lovely, almost beatific smile, and again he felt that ache inside; but this time it was a pleasing ache, not a desperate one.

He gathered her in his arms and held her close once more, kissed her on the nose and then lay back with a smile.

"The night of all nights," he said, "the very best night of all."

They both chuckled at that.

"Was it as good as you thought it might be?" Desiree asked.

"Better," he replied. "A thousand times better."

"Good sex?" Her grin was mischievous.

"Very good sex," he laughed, and hugged her.

There was a knock at the door. "Monsieur Colonel? I have breakfast for both of you."

"Dear Severine," Desiree murmured into his chest, "always prepared for every contingency."

"Indeed," Hans smiled. "Come in then, Severine!"

Severine entered with one large tray filled with a hearty breakfast for two; eggs, bacon, croissants, jam, coffee. It smelt heavenly to Desiree, who could barely remember eating anything the night before; she was usually so busy when she catered an event that she rarely ate anything herself.

But despite her hunger, Desiree felt incredibly good, almost buoyant, her body and soul both completely relaxed and at peace. She looked at Hans. He appeared just as relaxed and at peace. She'd never seen him so warm and so open.

"You've outdone yourself, Severine," he told the older woman as he admired the sumptuous repast. "Is it not a beautiful morning?" His voice was full of good cheer.

"I think perhaps for you two it is an exceptionally beautiful morning, M. Colonel," Severine replied with a wink. "Shall I pour coffee for you?"

Hans laughed. "Please do, thank you."

Once Severine had left, Hans got out of bed and Desiree admired his nude form as he walked across the room to retrieve his robe. He began to put it on.

"No, not yet," she breathed.

Hans turned and nearly trembled when he caught her admiring gaze.

"When you look at me like that, it drives me wild," he told her.

"You're so beautiful," she said.

"I'm not, really."

"Yes you are. You don't know how beautiful you are."

"No, it's you. You're the beautiful one. And I won't have you arguing with me on that point." He put on the robe and tied it round his waist. He reached over and grabbed his dress shirt from the night before.

"Here, wear this," he said, tossing it to her. "Otherwise I don't believe I'll make it through breakfast."

Desiree giggled, pulled on the shirt and joined him at the small table.

"It looks much better on you than it does on me," Hans told her with a wink.

"It's very soft."

"I have all my shirts made from the finest Egyptian cotton," he told her as he handed her one of the cups of coffee. "They're soft as butter, yet very, very sturdy. That shirt will last forever."

"Always the height of fashion." There was a mischievous note in her voice.

"Could I be anything less?" He grinned broadly, then ducked when Desiree tossed a morsel of bacon at him.

He watched her as they ate together. He had wondered if he could love her. He knew now that he already did, and irrevocably so. And he was happy; no longer frightened and hesitant. But with that love came an almost primal need to fully possess her, to protect her, to keep her with him always. And as he watched her spread jam on a croissant, he felt the sharp stab of desire in his belly once more. But with it came an ache of a different kind.

He wanted to keep her with him, but he knew that wouldn't be possible. Not if he wanted to save her. He could already feel the gnawing pain of losing her grow within him, but he pushed it down deep. It was necessary, but it didn't change his love for her. If nothing else, she would be with him as much as possible before she had to leave. That he couldn't deny himself.

"I wish I could keep you here, with me," he told her.

Desiree smiled with a touch of sadness. "You know that's impossible. It wouldn't keep me any safer, and it would only endanger you."

"I'm not talking just about that," he said sharply. "I'm talking about…"

Hans stopped himself before he said too much, and glanced away from those large, brown eyes with their inquiring gaze.

"I understand," Desiree said, finally. "I want it, too. But it can't happen."

He looked up and their eyes locked. His eyes were both warm and sad. Desiree could see that something had come to life inside him as a result of their night together. She knew it had for her as well. But that feeling was for both of them tempered by the bittersweet knowledge that, whatever they might dream of or hope for or want for the two of them, it could never happen.

Hans saw the change come over her face, and grew solemn himself.

"I've been working on a way to get you out of Europe," he told her.

"It's complicated, but it can be done."

"I know."

He looked at her sharply. "And how do you know this?" But then he shrugged and looked away.

"I know it's foolish of me to even ask, isn't it? But never mind, in the end it's not important, anyway. Knowing what I do about the possibilities for leaving Europe in this time of war, I imagine the plan is quite similar. There are simply different routes followed by our occupying forces and your resistance forces. Our route happens to be a great deal safer, but the end destination is the same.

"I can get you papers; legitimate ones that will get you through France and Spain to Portugal, where you can embark on a ship to America."

Desiree swallowed and nodded, and Hans caught the delicate movement in her throat as she did so.

"I'll make sure you're kept safe throughout the entire process. That's one thing I can do."

He reached over the table to take her hand, and looked deep into her eyes.

"It will have to happen quickly," he went on, "by the end of this week; perhaps sooner, if possible." Just saying the very words filled his soul with pain, but it was necessary.

***

Severine left them alone, only fetching their breakfast dishes, bringing them lunch, then dinner. She knew it was best to leave two lovers alone, especially these two, and especially at this time and in this place. Desiree and the Colonel needed to talk to each other. Severine sensed that they were both very wounded people, and maybe two wounded people could help each other heal. She hoped so.

She hadn't known Desiree long at all, but she felt the woman was right for the Colonel, and that he was right for her. Let them have what happiness they could. The odds were so much against them; and not the least of these odds was, she suspected, each other. But Severine had seen a great deal over the years, and she'd learned long since that there was very little that could be predicted in life.

Hans and Desiree talked and talked and talked. Everything in their pasts came pouring out, the differences; the similarities. The pain and the anger and love they'd each experienced in their lives. Desiree learned about Jürgen, and she understood; that was another enormous load lifted from Hans's shoulders. Of course she understood personally how desperate the need for love could be. Hans learned about Uwe, and he understood. He even understood the element of power play and pain Desiree had experienced in that relationship. It was not unfamiliar to him, after all.

Under other circumstances, he might have been her Uwe and perhaps, in one sense, he was. He suspected that part of what had drawn her to that man was not just the sense of a shared soul, but a shared darkness. It was what Hans felt for her as well, and what he knew she felt for him. Perhaps that was what love was, after all. Knowing the darkness in each other and not being afraid of it.

They made love twice more before she finally left the townhouse that evening, both times with a mixture of hunger and desperation. The first time she leaned over the bathroom counter and he entered her from behind so they could watch themselves together in the mirror and literally see what they were feeling. The urgency was almost unbearable, and they both came with violent intensity. Desiree sobbed, and Hans sobbed with her.

The second time was powerfully intense as well, but in a very different way. They clung to each other, rocked together; rained each other with hungry kisses. Desiree's head fell back and she gasped when she came. Hans bent over and slid his tongue into her open mouth, and when she suckled on it he shuddered and came with a harsh, raw groan.

***

"I don't want you to go," Hans whispered to Desiree after she'd dressed. He was holding her close to him, cradling her head against his chest.

"I have to; we both know I have to."

"Come back tomorrow evening, please. There's so much more we need to do, to talk about…"

"I will. I promise."

Hans came down the stairs with Desiree when she was ready to leave. He was once again wrapped in his robe; he hadn't bothered to dress that day.

Severine stepped out of the kitchen when she heard them.

"Good night Severine," Desiree told her. "I'll be back tomorrow."

Severine didn't say anything, but impulsively she drew the younger woman into a quick hug. She drew back and laid a hand along Desiree's cheek, then gave her an encouraging smile before she returned to the kitchen.

Desiree turned to give Hans a last kiss. They kissed for quite a while; neither wanted to let go. Finally, Hans reluctantly pulled away. He gave her a light smack on her bottom.

"Now be off with you," he said, "before I drag you back upstairs again."

Desiree grinned, then turned and went out the door. When it closed behind her, Hans's face fell. Tomorrow seemed very, very far away.

Chapter Fourteen

The phone was ringing when Desiree walked into her cottage. She ran to pick it up.

"So, you're home at last. I've been calling all day."

"Mathieu…"

"I wanted to make sure you were all right."

"I'm fine." And she was; more than he could know.

"I've spoken with Rene."

"What? What did he tell you?" Desiree was suddenly on full alert again.

"He didn't have to tell me anything. I knew already."

"Not over the telephone, Mathieu. It's not…"

"I know. Another time."

"Yes."

There was a pause before Mathieu spoke again: "You spent the night with him, didn't you?"

Desiree didn't answer. There was no way Matheiu could have understood.

"That's fine. I've no business even asking you."

"It's going to be all right," she told him. "Don't worry."

Mathieu gave a bitter chuckle. "You know, of course, that I always will wherever you're concerned."

After she'd hung up, Desiree looked around her small cottage. She had lived here for nearly fifteen years, and the idea of leaving the home and the life she'd made for herself here was daunting. Of course it wasn't as if she hadn't had to start over before. It seemed as though her entire life had been a series of fits and starts, the latter almost always new ones. But this was the place she'd lived the longest after she'd finished school. This was truly home to her.

She gazed at the photos of her son Sasha that donned the walls. If she had to leave half her clothing she would make sure she took every single one of those photos. That and Sasha's beloved teddy bear, which she kept on her bedside table.

Desiree suddenly felt very tired. She undressed and got into bed, but although she was sure she would fall asleep immediately, she found she couldn't. Lying naked in her bed suddenly felt deliciously lascivious. If she closed her eyes she could almost imagine Hans was there, sleeping quietly next to her. She could still smell him on her flesh; she hadn't wanted to shower before leaving his townhouse, she'd wanted to take that scent home with her.

Desiree found herself stroking the mattress, thinking of the wonderful texture of his skin on that lovely, small body of his. She felt pleasantly sore down below, yet also curiously empty; she was already yearning for Hans, and she slid a hand between her legs and idly stroked herself, until, at last, she fell asleep.

When she dreamt that night, she dreamt of Hans; of being held and kissed by him. Yet somehow she sensed that Uwe was there, too and that he was smiling.

***

Hans began working on obtaining Desiree's papers the very next day. The Obergruppenführer was pleased with the capture of the smugglers, and when Hans had made the request he didn't question it. He'd made the reasonable assumption that Hans had hoped he would, that Hans had made a deal with Desiree for the names in exchange for her exit visa.

The Obergruppenführer was wise enough not to ask about it; he knew better than to question Hans's methods and, as long as the capture had been made, the ring broken, what difference did it make, anyway? Certainly none to him.

This was why Hans had to get Desiree away quickly. Once the resistance got word of a deal, her life would be in far greater danger.

It was a risk he had to take. There was no other way to ensure her safe escape. At this point only he, Desiree and the Obergruppenführer knew that Hans had played a part in the capture of the smugglers. If any outsiders were to find out, there would be hell to pay, no mistaking it.

***

Sturmbannführer Dieter Strasser was going through some files for a particular case when he stumbled across a photo of the woman he knew as Aimienne. He took a look at the file, and light dawned; he knew that Faber's investigative techniques were often unorthodox, to say the least, but he hadn't expected them to be this unorthodox.

Strasser smiled at the photo before clipping it back in the file and closing the drawer. He knew he wasn't as clever as Faber, but he was certainly capable of holding his own. There might very well be something to gain from this knowledge, and far be it for him to overlook such an opportunity.

***

Desiree had already begun packing when the thought hit her. Hans was certainly capable of obtaining her exit visa and all the necessary papers, as well as making all the arrangements for her escape. But what would Mathieu, and Rene, think when she left town so quickly? They'd think she was responsible for the arrests, and they would hate her forever for it.

Should she tell them Hans was helping her to escape? No, that would make her look even worse. She was sure that they'd think that his help came in exchange for her betrayal.

What on earth could she tell them? Or should she tell them anything? Rene was also looking for a way to smuggle her out but, as Hans had rightly pointed out, it was unlikely that his way would be anywhere near as safe as having legitimate papers. After all, she had two borders to cross before she would make it to a ship.

Perhaps she should take it anyway. The war would end at some point, and she might want to come back here someday. She didn't want to burn her bridges behind her. But that wasn't the only reason. Mathieu and Rene had been loyal friends to her for so many years she couldn't bear the idea of them thinking of her as a collaborator.

Desiree took a break from her packing to sit down and have a cognac. She had to think about what to do. So much rested on this decision; it was as though all of her life was converging on this moment; past, present, and future, and all would be equally affected by the outcome.

***

Hans had sent Hermann out for a long lunch with instructions to bring lunch back for him, so he was a little surprised when he heard the outside office door open. His hand came to rest on his Walther almost instinctively as he rose from his chair.

"Standartenführer Faber?"

It was Strasser; no need to worry after all. Strasser was crafty and ambitious, but relatively harmless. In fact, Hans was convinced that the man had a bit of a crush on him based on the occasional longing glance he had caught. He certainly knew that Strasser looked up to him, if nothing else, and this was something that could prove very, very useful if needed.

"Come in, Sturmbannführer."

Strasser entered and saluted. "Heil Hitler!"

"Heil Hitler," Hans responded impatiently. "And what brings you out here today? I don't often see you here in 'my neck of the woods,' as the American cowboys would say."

"First, I wanted to thank you personally for the wonderful reception on Saturday." Strasser looked Faber straight in the eye as he said it.

Faber knew instantly he was up to something. After all, Strasser was every bit a predator like himself; he never uttered a word or made a move of any kind without a purpose.

"You're most welcome, but wouldn't a telephone call or note have sufficed?"

"I wanted to thank you personally."

"Obviously, since you're standing in my office doing just that."

Strasser smiled. He removed his cap and took off his gloves. He knew Faber disliked him; most people disliked him, which was rarely a concern to him.

"Planning to stay awhile, I take it," Faber said.

"Yes. I'm curious about something." Dieter liked to be coy, although he knew it displeased others.

"And what would that be?"

"Your caterer. I was going through some files today and came across a photo of her."

"You 'came across' her photo." Faber didn't believe it for a minute.

"Yes. That night, I didn't tell you that I'd met her before. I didn't think it was necessary."

Faber's brow lifted. He wasn't about to let on the sudden turmoil he was feeling at that moment.

"And when and where did you meet her?"

Strasser shifted a little uncomfortably. "In the town where I'm staying," he replied. "It's only a couple of towns away from here. I met her there around the time of the arms delivery." Strasser took a deep breath, and then looked directly at Faber. He was beginning to feel a little unnerved; this wasn't quite going the way he had thought it would.

"And? Where did you meet her?"

"In a tavern."

"A tavern." Faber brought a hand up to his chin, scrutinized Strasser more closely, who shifted uncomfortably at his steely gaze.

"I take it you bought her a drink," Faber went on.

"Yes, sir."

A malevolent smile spread across Faber's face, and Strasser felt a chill; he had seen that smile before.

"And then you took her home with you."

Strasser relaxed a bit. He was always happy to discuss his conquests, and it looked as though this was where the conversation was headed. He smiled.

"You saw how beautiful she is, sir."

"Indeed. And you didn't feel she was a bit old for you?"

Surprisingly, Strasser's face softened a little. "No sir," he said. He looked into the distance and his expression grew more thoughtful. "I didn't. She was lovely."

Faber's smile vanished, and his eyes grew icy. He rose from his desk and crossed round in front of it. Strasser was still looking into the distance; he hadn't seen the sea change that had come over the Standartenführer's countenance.

"You wanted her," Faber said, "so you took her home, and into your bed."

Strasser looked back into Faber's eyes, and he smirked. "Why not?"

In an instant, he knew that was a mistake. He was shoved up against the wall, both of Faber's hands around his neck. His breath was cut off; he tried to reach for Faber's wrists but suddenly found himself pulled to the ground, Faber's hands still tight around his throat. Faber knelt over him, one leg on either side of his body, and sat down; Strasser tried to grab at his arms, to buck him off, but without success. Faber leaned in and squeezed harder, putting all of his body weight into it.

"All I need do," he began, his voice low and steady, "is press a little harder," his hands tightened around Strasser's throat, his thumbs pressing deeper into the soft flesh, "and I could crush your esophagus," Faber finished.

Strasser struggled for breath, desperately clawed at Faber's arms as he fought to get some air into his lungs. His mouth moved, unleashed a high-pitched, frightened little sound as he gulped and tried to force some air through his windpipe. He could feel himself growing weaker, but he fought back his panic.

Faber drank in that panic, and felt the same heady exhilaration he'd experienced years ago when he'd last killed a man in this way. There was something powerfully primal in drawing the life from a man simply through the use of his hands. It aroused him tremendously in every fiber of his being. That his victim was a young, ridiculously pretty SS Sturmbannführer only made it more exciting.

Strasser's face was bright red as he struggled, swollen in horror, his soft mouth distorted. Seeing that made Faber hard. It made him very, very hard; especially when he saw that swollen face turn blue and the boy's grip weaken. He could kill this worthless piece of shit, kill him now and have it over with, take the body, bury it in the forest; but to what end? It clearly wasn't worth the trouble. Strasser certainly wasn't worth the trouble. What was he, after all? Nothing; less than nothing, in fact.

Slowly Faber loosened his grip, heard Strasser choke and gasp for air, and then his mind was lit with a new idea, a new pleasure. Just as Strasser was sure he was going to let up completely, Faber tightened his grip once more. The look of shock and terror on Strasser's face excited Faber immensely; it excited him so much he was on the verge of climaxing without even touching himself.

But then Faber began loosening his grip for good, and reason slowly began to return to his mind. He had much more important things to attend to than murdering a fellow (albeit junior) officer, and then having to contend with an investigation and all the nonsense that went with it. He was more than familiar with that, after all, and certainly wasn't interested in inviting it. Still, he kept his eyes on Strasser, savored the site of this arrogant young prick completely at his mercy. He watched the near-purple bloom in Strasser's cheeks fade to a pale pink, listened to his panting and wheezing.

Finally, Faber let go altogether, releasing Strasser, who coughed and took several deep gulps of air. Faber watched him closely as he waited for him to calm down and regain himself.

"As you can see, Sturmbannführer," he said, "I have no patience for impertinence."

"Ja, mein Herr," Strasser rasped. "My apologies, mein Herr."

Faber rose up, stood over him, gazing down at him in disgust. "I will tell you this once, Sturmbannführer, and I expect not to have to tell you again. First, you will never, ever use that impertinent tone of voice with me again. Second, you will never, ever assume that I don't know the whereabouts of a suspect at any given time, on any given day. And third, you will never, ever again presume that you have anything to offer me in a case without my asking you first. Now, is that clear?"

"Ja, mein Herr," Strasser croaked. He rose to his knees, looked up at his superior, and that was when Faber saw it; the very obvious indication that Strasser was just as aroused as he.

Faber's eyes blazed. He cocked his head, lifted a brow. "My goodness," he said, lifting a booted toe to contemptuously nudge the swelling in Strasser's trousers. "You enjoyed that little tussle between us, didn't you?"

Strasser blushed and looked down.

"Look at me," Faber commanded.

The Sturmbannführer raised his head in time to see the Standartenführer squeeze the bulge in his own trousers.

Faber watched the ripple of emotion cross Strasser's face; saw the look in his eyes change from fear and intimidation to one of hunger and desire.

"How very illuminating our little encounter has been," Faber said. "And how very valuable, wouldn't you agree? For both of us."

Strasser gazed up at him in surprise and wonder, and slowly rose to his feet, dusting off his leather coat. Faber smiled. The almost beatific look on the Sturmbannführer's face reminded him of someone; who? Ah, yes, the rent boy in the alley. Another creature he'd used solely for his personal satisfaction.

"And now that we know each other a little better," Faber continued, "perhaps we ought to socialize a little more often."

"Ja, Herr Standartenführer," Strasser responded, eyes still wide.

Faber's smile remained, but it began to lose its warmth, and grew increasingly stony.

"Now get out of my sight," he calmly told Strasser.

"Ja, mein Herr," Strasser came quickly to attention and saluted. "Heil Hitler!"

Faber returned the salute dismissively. Strasser grabbed his cap and gloves and made swift his departure.

Faber sat down behind his desk again. He might have made good the appearance of composure for Strasser's benefit, but inside his emotions were still in turmoil. The fury he'd felt toward Strasser had been transformed into desire for the young man; a desire that there was no question he would pursue, but the jealousy remained.

At that moment he was suddenly struck with raw need for Desiree. That she had been with an insect like Strasser cut him to the quick and filled him with despair and an aching desire for her.

She's mine, he thought. Mine. No one else should ever touch her. He laughed softly at that last thought. Desiree would be gone by the end of the week. He would probably never see her again. She would have other men, and he? Well, he would have Strasser, at least and many others, men and women, he was sure of it.

Still, he could barely stand the thought of her leaving him.

Chapter Fifteen

The food Hermann had brought back for Hans's lunch might as well have been straw for all the flavor it had for him. The hunger he felt wasn't for food, after all. Nor was it the raw hunger of sexual desire. No, it was that deeper hunger, the one that had haunted him all his life and the one that he felt could only be assuaged by Desiree.

He was tempted to leave his office, to drive out to her cottage to see her. At that moment he needed her more than he could ever imagine needing anyone in his life. But reason stepped in once more. There was no point in going to see her and further stirring up the turmoil inside him. He would see her soon enough, after all, that very night. It was far more important that he work on the details of her departure, even though it meant her exit from his life.

At heart, Faber had always been a practical man. He had always done what needed to be done; what he had to do. When it came to the practical matters of accomplishing a task, securing Desiree's safe exit was no different to him than carrying out any order he received from his command. There would always be that part of him that could effectively separate emotion from the action at hand.

He'd been well acquainted with this aspect of his personality for as long as he could remember. It had always been at the core of his success in any endeavor he took on. And he knew he could rely on it to sustain him through this one; the one he hated more than any other.

***

Desiree was surprised at how much she had managed to put together for her departure. But then it wasn't really that much; she was to leave suddenly, after all, to simply vanish, so it wasn't as though she had much to pack. Only the essentials would come; some clothing, her camera, her photos of Sasha, and a few other things. Everything else would be left behind. All of her past would be left behind as she embarked on a new life.

Her business was another question. She had clients who depended on her, after all. She had to make suitable arrangements for them to continue to receive the service they'd come to rely upon. Desiree would make the rounds to take her orders today, as she always had, then pass on those orders to Jean & Anne-Marie Antoinelle, who ran a business similar to hers. They would fill the orders, make the deliveries, take over her catering; they would essentially assume a business that had kept Desiree's life comfortable, if simple, but would most certainly enrich theirs, and she was glad of that.

Desiree left her cottage, order book in hand, to make that final round to all her clients. The last one on her list, as always, was Rene. She still wasn't sure how much, if anything, she would tell him, but she felt compelled to tell him something.

As she drove towards her first client, the small grocery in Angouleme, Desiree reflected on the value of that compulsion to reveal all to Rene. Perhaps Mathieu would be better. He, after all, had known her far longer, and unlike Rene, he wasn't in love with her. He loved her, that was true, but not the way she felt Rene clearly did. And Mathieu would be able to explain the circumstances to Rene in a way he could understand without being hurt, which would surely happen if she herself explained it.

Desiree turned her truck down a street away from the grocery, to M. Guidon's estate and to Mathieu.

***

Mathieu had been thinking and worrying about Desiree all day. There was something odd at work here, and he couldn't quite pinpoint what it was. He hadn't expected to be as shaken as he was by her having spent the night with that SS Colonel. But then she was too close to the operations, too much a part of the process for him to feel comfortable with her doing so.

And then there were the arrests, of course. Guy had been tortured, but he hadn't talked. He'd been imprisoned, and there was word that he and the others would be sent to one of the camps in the East rather than executed; although few people seemed to return from these camps.

Mathieu realized he would have to face the unpleasant possibility that Desiree was a collaborator. It seemed unthinkable, but perhaps it was true. It wouldn't be long before he had the chance to confront her about it. She was due in less than an hour to take his weekly order.

He was startled by the familiar honk of her horn outside. She was early this week, which surprised Mathieu. He knew she always stopped at the grocery first, and for years now he had been able to track her arrival nearly to the minute. Something was obviously different today.

Not to mention that usually he could hear her truck coming up the long drive, but he'd been too distracted to do so this time. He went to the door to let her in, and they greeted each other warmly. Desiree was deceptively business-like, and began taking his order immediately.

Mathieu listed all the items he needed while she wrote them down. He couldn't take his eyes off her the entire time. She was flushed, her hair tousled around her shoulders, and she looked utterly lovely. He was suddenly filled with sadness for all he might have had with this woman he had loved so much; indeed, that he still loved, although now in a way quite different than he loved his wife, Mariette. He had a life with Mariette, after all. He had built with her the life he'd wanted to build with Desiree, a life that included three children he adored.

But Mathieu had given more of himself to Desiree than he had to any other woman in his life, even Mariette. He'd opened his heart to her in a way he'd never done before or since. In that sense she was his true love, the one that couldn't possibly last but would, and did, shape all the others in his life.

He gave the last of his order, and he watched as she closed her order book and faced him directly, a solemn look on her face.

"I have to speak with you, Mathieu. It's very important. That's why I came here before stopping at the grocery."

"I think I know," he replied.

Desiree looked at him in surprise.

"You have something to tell me…something about the arrests of Guy and the others."

She blushed and ducked her head, and he was suddenly filled with rage.

"Did you betray them, Desiree? Tell me."

Something about the word "betray" got to Desiree. Her head bolted back up in shock, and her eyes blazed. "Never," she replied. "How could you think such a thing?"

"How could I think it? You spent Saturday night with the Colonel we now know is in charge of the investigation. The very night after they were all arrested."

"Yes," she said, holding her gaze steady, although inside she felt as though she were trembling from head to toe. "I did. And he told me then that he'd been sent to seduce me as part of that investigation."

Now it was Mathieu who was shocked. "He told you that?"

"Yes. Because he knew I'd be suspected by all of you once the arrests were made. He didn't get any information from me, I swear it. He didn't want to get it from me. He didn't want anything to happen to me."

And with that, Desiree began to cry. Damn it, why was she always so prone to tears around Mathieu and Rene? It didn't really matter, however, because Mathieu immediately pulled her into his arms and held her close. He stroked her hair as she wept against him.

It seemed insane to Mathieu, and yet somehow it all made sense. He didn't quite understand how or why, but it did make sense. After all, Desiree's life had never followed any common or recognizable trajectory. Perhaps she was never meant to lead what one would call an "ordinary" life.

Mathieu reached for a kitchen towel and brought it up to wipe away her tears, smiling as he did so. How many tears had he mopped from her cheeks over the years he'd known her? More than he could ever count. He smiled. Perhaps this was the role he was ultimately destined to play in her life, and it wasn't an unimportant one.

Desiree looked up at him, and Mathieu gently pressed the towel against the damp spots beneath her eyes.

"I think…he cares for me, Mathieu." She wanted him to understand.

"That doesn't surprise me. And do you, for him?"

"Yes," she replied without hesitation.

"Do you love him?"

Desiree was silent for a while.

"Yes," she finally said, quietly.

"So what happens now?"

"I have to leave. He's making the arrangements."

Mathieu looked at her curiously, and then his expression hardened.

"This Nazi is making arrangements for you to leave, and yet you say you had nothing to do with the arrests."

Desiree stepped back from him and pinned him with a fierce glare.

"Absolutely not," she snapped. "Never."

"Then how did he find out where to go, whom to arrest?"

"I don't know. He wouldn't tell me."

Mathieu stood quiet for a moment, deep in thought.

"Don't you see, Mathieu? He got the information on his own. He didn't want to use me to do to it, because in the end he would have had to arrest me."

"He's not arresting you, and he's able to make arrangements for you to leave. Don't you see, Desiree? Whether or not you said anything, he wants to make it seem as though you did. I'm sure he has to just to get you the papers you'll need. How else would he be able to get you out of the country? You tell me!"

"Don't you think I know that? That's why I'm telling you!!"

They were both silent at that.

"Why else would I have told you all of this?" Desiree went on. "Why would I even tell you anything at all if I had betrayed everyone? Wouldn't I just disappear, instead?"

"That makes sense," Mathieu nodded. "That makes a great deal of sense."

"And I need your help for the very last time," she added. "I need you to explain things to Rene after I've gone."

"And your business? I assume you'll be taking orders the rest of the afternoon, as usual."

"I'm selling it. All today's orders will be fulfilled and delivered by the Antoinelles. Don't worry about it, and don't say a word to anyone. After I've left, you can explain things to Rene.

Mathieu looked at Desiree closely. "I understand," he said. "I'll do as you've asked."

"Merci, mon ami."

"This is the last time I'll see you, isn't it?"

"Yes," Desiree said softly.

"Then come here."

She moved closer to him and Mathieu pulled her into a strong embrace, his last embrace, and kissed her. He had forgotten what it felt like, his lips on hers, how soft they were; how sweet it was. He kissed her with every fiber of his being, and all of it was in that kiss, their past, their present, his life with his family, her unknown future.

There was love, too, in that kiss; a love that had taken a different direction than he'd originally wanted, but it was still love and still strong nevertheless. And there was sadness; the sadness of two close friends parting in a time of war, two friends almost certain they would never see each other again.

But when they finally drew apart, Desiree and Mathieu smiled at each other. They'd both felt all of it in that kiss, and they both understood it. With that understanding, came a kind of peace between the two of them, whatever might happen next.

Mathieu reached up to lay a hand on Desiree's cheek, and she leaned into it affectionately.

"Au revoir," he said softly.

"Au revoir," she replied. She lingered for only a moment, then turned and left. He went to the door, watched her get into her truck. She started the engine, then turned to him once more.

He smiled at her and waved.

She smiled back, waved at him in return, then started up the long drive. Mathieu stood in the doorway for a while after Desiree's truck finally disappeared. At that very moment, a chapter of his life was coming to a close. He was losing someone who had been very, very important to him. It seemed right to pause for a moment to think about that person.

Mathieu stood there for a few minutes more, gazing into the distance, watching the last of the dust settle after Desiree's departure. Then he turned, closed the door, and went back to his work.

There was a meal to prepare, after all. There was always a meal to prepare.

Chapter Sixteen

Hans was silent as Hermann drove him back to his townhouse. He'd begun putting the plan in motion for Desiree's departure, and things were going well. But there was a deep ache inside him that wouldn't subside; in fact, couldn't subside, not until he saw her again.

It was one great ache made up of all the pain inside him, the pain of being an abandoned child, of feeling so alone for so much of his life, of not being able to tell the one person who loved him most that he loved him in return. It was the pain of knowing that the woman he loved had been with someone else, the pain of knowing that he would lose her soon, and that he would likely never see her again.

Faber gave Hermann a brusque nod as he got out of the car. He was tired; it had been a long day, after all. When he entered the townhouse, Severine came out of the kitchen to take his coat and cap.

"Dinner will be ready within an hour," she said. "Are you all right, sir?"

"I'm fine," he answered, "just tired. I'll be in the parlor having a drink. When Desiree arrives, please show her in."

"Oui, M. Colonel."

Hans entered the parlor, unbuttoned his tunic and dropped it carelessly on one of the armchairs. All day the cloth had felt heavy on him, somehow weighing down his movements, slowing him. He fixed himself a vodka on the rocks from a bottle purloined from a recent deportation.

Of course it was heavy, he thought. His work, though frequently enjoyable, especially when the puzzles he was assigned to solve proved especially challenging, could just as often be terribly burdensome. Never had this been truer than when he was assigned to this case with Desiree.

And in the end, had it even been worth it? She had fucked Strasser.

Strasser, for Christ's sake. Never mind the boy himself. After all, he'd learnt enough about him that afternoon to control and manipulate him for years to come, and Faber had every intention of doing just that. It would certainly afford him a great deal of pleasure, both physical and psychological. He would take and take and take from the boy, drain him and bend him entirely to his will, make him depend on him for everything before casting him aside; and that would be revenge enough.

But it was different with Desiree. It wasn't revenge he wanted from her, but rather to re-stake his claim to her. He had to know she was still his because he wanted her, needed her so much. It was nearly unbearable, that want and that need, and yet somehow it was a beautiful agony.

The parlor doors opened, and she was here at last. She closed the doors behind her.

Hans got up and crossed over to Desiree immediately, pulled her into his arms and kissed her roughly, passionately, instilling all of his soul into that hungry, desperate kiss, and she returned it with equal passion.

Her mouth seemed sweeter than ever, and that sweetness flooded him, suffused his limbs, made him feel light and on air and yet also powerfully strong, as though he could do anything, best any man, win any challenge, conquer any country. Her tongue met his, and he could feel her strength as well, and her passion, and it felt like they were feeding these feelings to and from each other, making them both even stronger.

Hans shoved Desiree against the wall, dropped his suspenders, lifted her skirt and tore at her underwear. She reached down to help him undo his trousers.

He lifted her, braced her against the wall and drove deep inside her; they shared a mutual groan of pleasure and relief. She wrapped her legs around his waist and he gripped her behind, held her in place as he thrust in and out. She threw her head back against the wall and whimpered while he licked at her lips, her face, her ear, and her throat, then bit into the soft flesh there.

He stifled her cry by covering her mouth with his. It was good, so good, good beyond belief, and when he felt her get close, he held on, gripped her harder, drove into her deeper, kissed her wildly, and as soon as he felt her let go he came apart and pulled her even closer to him, driving deep inside her, as deep as he could go, until he let loose with his own sharp cry and bit into her throat once more.

Afterwards, they very nearly collapsed, they were both so undone, and at the same time they both felt lightheaded and giddy, and they started to laugh together. Hans pulled Desiree to him and hugged her tightly, and she held him just as tightly and kissed him deeply, and as they kissed Hans mind raced with a single thought; I need you, I need you, I need you, I love you.

I love you. He still couldn't say it, but he felt it now, stronger than ever, vivid and bright inside him, more powerful than anything else he'd ever known. There was pleasure and serenity mixed in with that feeling, more serenity than he'd ever experienced before. And all of it had meaning to him. All of it made sense; even the damned crazy world made sense at that very moment.

***

Severine brought their supper into the parlor so they could relax together on one of the sofas. It was a colorful and sumptuous repast; chicken, mushrooms, green beans, carrots, potatoes, white wine and, later, for dessert, the most cunning little heart-shaped cakes with pink frosting, freshly baked that very afternoon. Severine blushed when she served them with the coffee, and Hans's brow lifted.

"If I didn't know better," he said as he reached for one of the cakes, "I'd say you were becoming quite the romantic, Severine."

"I'm afraid I got a little carried away," she said sheepishly. "Forgive me."

Hans handed a cake to Desiree, then took another for himself and bit into it.

"From the taste of this, there's nothing to forgive," he told her with a smile, and Severine grinned broadly as she left the room.

Hans took his coffee, leaned back against the sofa and pulled Desiree against him. "Tell me what you did today," he said.

She told him of packing, of taking her orders, of making the arrangements for her business. It had been a difficult day for her. Hardest of all had been taking Rene's order without being able to say anything to him. He told her that his contacts had called him to report that things were going well in the plans for her escape. Of course she mentioned none of this to Hans.

Desiree looked into Hans's eyes as she spoke. They were different, somehow. They were still lit with a special light mixed with sadness; but the quality of that sadness had changed.

Hans was only half-listening as he gazed at her. She was so beautiful.

He couldn't ignore the pain he felt over the fact that Strasser had touched her, kissed her, made love to her; but should he say anything about it?

Hans was surprised that he was even asking himself this question. He was a man of action, after all. Never in his life had he hesitated to take action when it was warranted, and rare was the occasion when it wasn't.

But for some odd reason he was hesitant to do so now.

How foolish of him.

"I had a visitor today," he began.

"Did you," Desiree responded, puzzled by his abruptness.

"Major Dieter Strasser paid me a call," Hans continued. "I understand you've met him before."

Desiree blushed, and looked down.

"I saw him once," she said.

"Look at me."

Desiree looked up. His jaw was set, firm. His eyes blazed with a look of anger mixed with despair, which only toughened her resolve. She sat up and looked right into those eyes when she spoke.

"I saw him once," she said firmly. "We both understood it wasn't going to happen again."

Hans took a deep breath. "He wanted it to," he said.

"I know he did. But he also realized it wasn't going to happen again. And that night at the townhouse he realized it for good."

They were both silent for a moment. Hans's eyes still blazed, but Desiree's steady gaze never wavered.

"I want you," Hans finally said. "I don't want anyone else to have you."

Desiree took his hand and held it. "I know," she said, "I know."

Hans smiled. "Of course it's idiotic of me," he told her. "You'll leave, I'll never see you again, and you'll have other men."

"And you'll have other women - and men."

Hans fell silent. Of course she was right. She couldn't have been more right, especially with Strasser waiting in the wings.

"Don't you see how foolish it is for either of us to fret over it?" Desiree went on. "We have so few days left. Let's not waste them."

Hans gazed deep into Desiree's beautiful, large brown eyes. There was so much more strength and serenity in those eyes than he could ever imagine feeling, and it terrified him to think just how weak she made him feel and how much he needed her. It was a need so powerful that it threatened to engulf him completely. What would he do when she had to leave? How would he live without those eyes, that strength and serenity—how would he live without her?

And then Desiree brought his hand up to her mouth and kissed it.

"I know how you feel," she said, her voice soft. "I feel it too, just as much as you do."

"I need you," he whispered. "I need you so, and that terrifies me."

And he pulled her to him, kissed her again with a wholly new ferocity and hunger, and she returned his kiss with the same.

Hans drew back; let his lips graze her face, her ear. He took her earlobe between his teach and tugged at it, gently, then let go again, let his lips brush against her ear.

"You've made me feel again," he whispered. "You've made me feel so much…"

***

He was deep inside her, lying against her, her legs wrapped around his legs, her hands clinging to his shoulders, and it was bliss - sheer bliss.

Hans had never before known what it was like to be so close to another human being, not even with Jürgen. He clung to Desiree, held her close, kissed her again and again, willed every ounce of feeling he had for her into her body and her soul.

It was exquisite to feel so much, to feel another human being, to be a part of her. He hadn't known it was possible, to be able to lose himself inside someone, to be adrift in another person's soul.

Desiree moaned beneath him and Hans joined her, and together they voiced their need and their passion, like two lone wolves baying at the moon. Hans reached down, grabbed her hips, and pulled her even closer to him. Where they were joined felt liquid and molten, the friction of even the slightest movement so pleasurable it was almost unbearable, and neither of them ever wanted it to end.

Hans captured Desiree's mouth, held it with his own, took her breath and her moans inside him while feeding his to her in turn. And then he couldn't hold it inside him any longer. He pulled his lips from her and moved his mouth back to her ear, to at last whisper it to her:

"Ich liebe dich…"

She understood him, and whimpered and clung to him even more tightly. He moved inside her, began to drive into her even deeper, and then he whispered it again, and again, almost like a chant, ich liebe dich, ich liebe dich, ich liebe dich; and when Desiree heard those familiar words relayed to her in another litany as powerful as the one she'd experienced so long ago, she pressed up against him very hard and sobbed, and came so powerfully that he couldn't help but follow, coming with equal force, emptying his very being inside her.

He stayed inside her as long as he could afterwards, kissing her tenderly on her lips, her face, her hair, and her throat. He brought a hand up to her cheek and held it, then smiled down at her. He was met with a smile so sweet it made him ache.

There had been so few times in Hans's life - most of them with Jürgen -that he had felt at peace. But he did now. He knew it wouldn't last. That kind of serenity never did, but he would savor every moment of it nonetheless. He would exult in it for as long as it did last. Life had a way of progressing on its own terms, with little thought to the people in its path; Hans had long since known that nothing was forever.

But now; now was perfect, a moment he could and would safely pocket into his memory and carry with him always. It wasn't much, but at the same time it was everything and it would sustain him for some time to come.

He leaned forward, then, and planted another tender kiss on those soft, full lips.

Chapter Seventeen

Their hands were together, palm to palm.

"Look how small your hand is," said Hans.

"It's not that much smaller than yours," Desiree teased.

"Yes, but mine is more rough-looking. Yours is more delicate."

"Delicate? With all those cuts and calluses?" Years of food preparation had left both her hands toughened and scarred.

"Yes. It's beautiful." He brought her hand to his mouth and kissed it, then let go of it to turn and run a hand across her belly, caressing it.

"You're not afraid of me," he murmured. There was a touch of wonder in his voice.

"No."

"You would be if you knew some of the things I've done."

"Like what? You've killed people? I never thought otherwise, and I still -"

she bit back the words, still hesitant to speak them.

"You still love me," he answered for her, surprising himself.

"Yes," she turned to him, "I love you."

"And I love you." He kissed her. "Ich liebe dich."

"I knew when you said it tonight. Uwe…" again she hesitated.

"Uwe said it to you."

"Yes. But I never said it back. I never told him, and…"

Hans gathered Desiree close to him. "I know. Jürgen said it to me but I couldn't say it back to him, either. Now he's on the Eastern Front, where your Uwe died, and I may never see him again."

Now it was she who kissed him, tenderly, to soothe him, and ran a calming hand through the hair on his chest.

"You made love with Jürgen."

"Yes. He was the only person I'd ever made love to; until you." Hans took hold of her hand again, laced it in his, and smiled at her.

"Did you..." she hesitated.

"Did we fuck? Yes. I took him inside me. He's the only man I've ever taken inside me. He's the only man I ever will let inside me." Hans stopped. Never say never, he thought. If there was anything he had learned in life, it was that.

"It's all right," Desiree said. "We both know that there are no absolutes in life aside from death."

"You've had men and women, just like me."

"Yes."

"You had a child with a man."

Desiree laughed. "Not quite. I got pregnant, not expecting it to happen, and although I wanted to keep my child, I had no interest in telling the father. I didn't want or expect anything from him. But when Sasha was two I realized it was unfair not to tell his father. I thought he should have the right to at least know of his son's existence, so I told him."

"And what happened?"

"Nothing. He wanted nothing to do with our son. He'd married by then, and had a child with his wife. He had no interest in disturbing the equilibrium of his life by introducing a child by another woman into it."

"Were you hurt by that?"

"Not really. Oh, for my son, at first, but then I'd never mentioned his father to him, not even when I contacted him. I felt it was better that he know nothing at all, than to know his father rejected him."

"That makes sense."

"Did you ever have children? I know you've never married."

"Not that I know of, and it's probably just as well. What kind of father could I have possibly been?"

"What do you mean?"

Hans was silent for a moment.

"I'm not like other men," he finally began. "There's too much...anger inside me. I would only bring harm to a child. Not physical harm, but up here." He tapped at his temple.

"A child changes you," Desiree told him. "You wouldn't have been the same person. A child takes your focus away from yourself in a way no other person can."

She was leaning over him now, still caressing the hair on his chest. She lowered her head and kissed one nipple. Hans closed his eyes for a moment to concentrate on the sensation of her tongue sweeping around it, then opened them again.

"My father…" he began, a little hesitantly, "well, I suppose I should call him that, but he didn't - he never wanted to - spend time with me when I was a child."

"He never talked with you, or played with you, or read to you?" Desiree asked.

"Never. I don't believe he or my mother really wanted children. They had me because that was what you did when you married; you had children. That was part of the bargain, as it were. But they were very deeply in love, very much absorbed in each other, and I was a distraction."

"I was seven when they sent me away to school," he continued. "For the next fifteen years, I rarely saw them. Oh, at Christmas, yes, but never any other time of year."

"You must have been so terribly lonely," Desiree said.

"I imagine so, but I never felt lonely. Had I not been sent away to school, I still would not have spent much time with my parents, so I had no one to feel lonely for. That's the way good Austrian children were raised back then. I never knew there was any other way to be."

Desiree looked into his eyes. "There is," she said. "There is."

She leaned over and kissed him deeply. Hans took her face in both his hands and met that kiss with equal passion.

Desiree pulled away and began planting kisses along his jaw line, then down his throat. Hans closed his eyes and sighed. The soft press of her lips against his flesh made him shiver with pleasure. It was a very light touch, almost like a dusting of feathers against his skin, but it held so much for him that it filled him with an almost unbearable joy. To be touched like this, to be so cherished, so loved. Perhaps he'd never quite grasped what loneliness was, but at that very moment a lifelong hunger was at last being assuaged.

Desiree kissed the hollow at the base of his throat, moved her lips along his collarbone. She kissed both his nipples, felt him tremble as her lips continued their path down his belly, pressed into his navel, traced the soft trail of hair down to his groin.

Hans moaned. He was getting hard again, and he ached to feel her mouth on him. His head tossed restlessly when he felt her nose and mouth rub against the curls of hair that surrounded his erection.

He trembled when she wrapped a hand around and gently began

stroking him, then loosened her grip to let her lips kiss their way reverently up his shaft.

Hans opened his eyes, watched her pull back his foreskin and slip her tongue lightly inside it; he shuddered violently at that oh-so-intimate touch, which took them both by surprise. His hands came down then, began to stroke her hair as her tongue encircled the very tip of his cock.

He felt that sweet tongue push back his foreskin, felt her mouth envelop and then move down his swelling cock, and it felt unbelievably intimate for her to take him this way, into her mouth, into her throat; that shudder was unwavering now as he felt himself drawn ever deeper into oblivion.

She could own him this way and did, drawing tremor after tremor from the very center of his being. He wanted to move his hips but she wouldn't let him, and then he felt it rising within him, something that promised the fiercest pleasure imaginable as it grew larger and larger into a painfully elusive almost, almost, almost - and then he was suddenly there, gripping her head, grinding his hips against her mouth with each sharp spasm, his own head flung back against the pillow as he let out a cry that ended in a sob.

He lost himself then. Engulfed in that deeply pleasing darkness, he let go, and was at last set free.

He came to only when he felt the brush of her lips against his throat, then his jaw, then his cheek; he opened his eyes then, and pulled her down into a kiss in which he tasted himself, and the ocean, and life.

***

He held her very, very close.

"What will I do without you?" he asked.

"You'll go on," she said. "We'll both go on with our lives."

"I don't want to. Not without you."

"Yes, you do, and you will. You must."

Hans closed his eyes, let Desiree kiss his cheek, again and again. He knew she was right. He would go on with or without her. He always had, after every loss he'd suffered, and he always would.

He wished it weren't so. With every fiber of his being he wished it. But it was so. He would never die for love, never have a noble end, but instead continue to drift through the lives of others, following whatever purpose was set before him. Why should his life be any different from all the other lives out there in the past, present and future?

But for now he could savor everything he felt for this woman, the sweet deliciousness of it, the need and the love he had for her. For now, he could hold her close to his heart, and at least pretend as though he never had to let her go.

***

"I have your papers ready for you," Hans told Desiree the next morning. "You'll leave on Friday."

He was standing beside her. She was still seated at their breakfast table. Once again he took her hand and kissed it.

"You'll have a courier for the first leg of your journey," he went on, "to take you through Spain to Portugal. Once across the border you'll have transportation to the port of Lisbon. You'll board a merchant steamer headed for New York.

"You'll have a little money when you arrive. Not much, but it should help you get started while you look for employment."

He was still holding her hand. She leaned against his waist and he brought his free hand over to stroke her hair.

"I love you." He said it simply, straightforwardly. "I'm doing this because I love you."

Hans pulled Desiree closer and let her wrap her arms around his waist. He chuckled, and she looked up at him. He shook his head, a wry grin on his face.

"I've never done anything for anyone before," he told her. "I simply haven't. I haven't lived for others. I've lived for myself alone. So this is an entirely new experience for me."

"How does it feel?"

He chuckled again, gazed down into her eyes, reached out to touch that soft cheek of hers.

"I won't lie to you," he replied, "It doesn't feel good. It fills me with rage. I want you here, with me. Always. I don't want to lose you."

They gazed deep into each other's eyes. His were tormented and despairing; hers were filled with sadness but also with strength; a strength that he hoped might be enough for both of them. He knelt beside her, wanting so desperately to find succor in that strength of hers.

"We're both pragmatic people," she told him. "We do what has to be done."

"I'm tired of it," Hans said. "I'm tired of doing what I have to do. But at this point," he stopped and sighed, "our lives aren't our own in these circumstances," he went on. "We don't have many choices to make.

"No, we don't," Desiree agreed. "I'm tired of it, too, but what else is there to do in a war but try to live? We have to view every single breath we draw as a victory; a victory over death."

***

A victory over death. But what a bitter victory it was. Hans held on to this thought when he made love to Desiree once more that morning, before they each left for the day. Somehow doing so made the pleasure even greater. And when he fed that pleasure to her he felt immensely strong; stronger and more powerful than he had ever felt before.

What had begun as the ache of lust and desire had grown into a mountain of intense, raw need, and it was bliss to feel that need and the love that came with it. To want someone so much and to feel how much she wanted him.

How could he have ever thought that he was incapable of feeling? Hans marveled at the thought when he was joined with Desiree, savoring even the most minute of sensations, finding incredible joy when he released his seed deep inside her. He had been afraid to feel before; now he never wanted not to.

It was the same for Desiree. Every motion of their bodies felt right. Each press of their flesh together brought a new revelation. This was not just physical and emotional pleasure but something infinitely more, something larger than both of them that consumed them completely.

They didn't hesitate to say it to each other now, to whisper it tenderly in each other's ear, to gasp it out at the moment of climax:

Je t'aime.

Ich liebe dich.

Chapter Eighteen

When Hermann drove him to the office that morning, Hans was silent, thinking about Desiree. It was becoming more and more difficult to part from her.

What a world this was, he thought, a wry smile playing on his lips; one that would withhold such joy from him for so long, only to allow him the briefest taste of it before withdrawing it again; and for good.

When he was with Desiree, Hans knew he was at his most vulnerable. But now, whenever he was parted from her, something within him hardened. Some already steely resolve was being made stronger and more potent by the deepening rage he was feeling. Her papers would arrive today. Everything was in order. She would be gone by the end of the week. Her life would be saved at the cost of losing her.

Hans shook his head and the wry smile grew. If he were a better person, he imagined, he would feel ennobled by what he was doing and live forever off the memories of his time with Desiree. But he was not and never would be a noble man. He was an angry and selfish man. As a child he'd never liked sharing his toys or his friends; at university he had found it very difficult when Jürgen spent time with other friends or with his girlfriends. Hans had always been possessive, and always would be.

He worked at his desk for some time before a memory suddenly hit him. That last night with Jürgen; or rather, very early that last morning, he had awoken eager to be taken once more and had, in turn, awakened Jürgen with hot, eager kisses. Jürgen had then turned him over roughly onto his belly so Hans could feel the press of Jürgen's hot flesh against his back, feel those strong, skillful hands move down his body and the press of his hard cock against his behind.

He had arched up to welcome Jürgen's erection, felt his tender embrace in response, and for one long, glorious moment, Hans gave himself up to that embrace, let the tenderness in it envelop him, body and soul.

Jürgen's body completely covered him; Hans felt his assured and gentle touch, the press of his lips against his throat, and then his hot breath in his ear as two well-lubricated fingers slid slowly inside him, stretching him once more, readying him for that final, beloved intimacy.

And then there was that familiar press of silken flesh against his entry, that slow push and their shared moan at that initial slide inside; that wonderful sense of being completely filled, completely taken, that made Hans push back eagerly and let loose with a low, keening wail.

It was so dark, so quiet. Jürgen wrapped one arm around Hans's waist, licked and bit at his ear, while with the other he braced himself against the mattress. He rocked his hips to move in deeper, and Hans rocked back to meet him, lost completely in the moment, wanting it to last forever; this incredible merging of their two beings. Jürgen increased his thrusts until they were almost savage, and finally a sharp cry erupted from his throat. He had never cried out before and Hans felt him spurt deep inside him. With that sensation Hans had let go more completely than he ever had before, coming with such force that he gasped and sobbed.

There was a sad, still moment afterwards when each of them had felt what the other was thinking; that this could very well be the last time they would ever make love. It was a memory Hans would always keep with him, because he now understood what it meant to be so close to someone that you could feel their thoughts as surely as you shared them. He understood what it meant to completely possess another person; mind, body and soul, and he also understood what it meant to be so possessed. He hadn't been able to fully recognize it before, but now Hans realized that he had experienced the same with Desiree. And suddenly, the need to do so again was almost overwhelming.

***

Desiree had packed everything she could take. It wasn't much; her camera, many of her photos, including all those of Sasha, her prep knives, and Sasha's precious teddy bear. The walls in her cottage, once covered with those photos, were now bare; leaving only ghosts of their former presence in the darker spots on the wallpaper they had once covered.

What makes a house a home? It was a question Desiree hadn't had much cause to ponder in her life. The places she'd lived in the past had never been permanent. But this cottage was different. She hadn't really thought about it, but she realized now that she had never expected to leave. She had spent fifteen years here, after all; longer than she'd ever lived anywhere else. She'd planted roots, certain that she would remain in this cottage for the rest of her life. Now she was being forced to uproot and move on.

This had also been the only home her darling Sasha had ever really known. He was far too young when they left Paris to ever remember the flat in which he'd been born. Leaving this cottage would be like leaving her child behind, and the very thought of doing so tore at her heart almost as horribly as his death had.

Desiree shivered when she thought of that terrible loss. Sasha's death had been like having a limb torn from her body. One of the most important parts of her had been destroyed, and it was still agonizing to think about. For years she kept herself as numb as possible to avoid thoughts of her lost child. If it meant she had to feel nothing at all, then it was better to do so than to suffer such incredible pain.

Desiree was glad now that there was no grave to leave behind. That would have made the pain even more acute. As difficult as it had been at the time, cremation had been the right choice. Mathieu had been right about that. They had scattered Sasha's ashes from the top of the hill outside of town, and she'd watched them dissolve and blow away. She found comfort in the thought that her child would somehow always be around her, in the wind and in the air.

Desiree had been numb for some time when Uwe reawakened her. As wrong as some might think it; and she thought it herself at first, the physical pain he subjected her to somehow helped her to break down and weaken the emotional pain. Uwe had helped her to feel again; he'd brought her senses back to life. And in sharing this experience with him, she had awoken the human, caring, compassionate part of his soul that had always lurked deep inside but had never before emerged. That was how Uwe had come to love her, and why Desiree had loved him in return, although she hadn't wanted to recognize it at the time.

Now there was Hans, whom she loved even more than she had loved Uwe. In a sense, she and Hans were both wounded souls who had somehow found something healing in each other. It couldn't make either of them whole; nothing would ever completely obliterate the scars left by past wounds. But it was enough to sustain Desiree's will to live. She hoped it would be enough for Hans as well. She couldn't help but worry how her departure might affect him. Would he shut himself down once more, become hardened again?

Desiree got up from the table where she had been sitting, walked to the door and opened it. She looked beyond the town to that very hill in the distance where she'd let Sasha go. Her child wasn't in the cottage itself, he was in the air, the very air around her; the air that would travel with her to America. And she had traces of him as well. Photos. The teddy bear. And something she'd found deep in a drawer, something she'd almost forgotten; the very first spoon with which she'd fed him when he was a baby, the same sterling silver spoon her mother had used to feed her, and that her grandmother had used to feed her mother. She had wrapped this spoon carefully in a silver cloth and packed it.

She would be forever grateful to Mathieu for understanding how important it would be for her to never feel that she was leaving Sasha behind. Her beloved child would be with her always, wherever she went in the world, until that day when her death would reunite them.

**

Hermann knocked on Hans's office door, entered when acknowledged, and handed him a sheaf of papers.

"These just came, sir. A report from Paris."

Faber took the papers and skimmed quickly through them. He'd half-expected this; the Resistance was planning to move on Desiree. He was suddenly fully alert, seized by a fiercely protective instinct that made his already predatory nature even stronger.

If he had to kill every one of them with his bare hands, he would do so. Every last one of them. No one would touch her.

"Hermann," he said, "bring the car around."

**

When he'd first been told, Rene had gone pale, unable to believe it. He'd asked for more information, and when he had heard it all, especially that she'd been bedding that murderous Colonel, the very one who'd given the order to capture Guy and the others, he got angry. Very angry.

All this time he'd loved a traitor, one of the worst of the collaborators, a woman who'd taken a Nazi into her bed, into her body and perhaps even into her heart. And she'd lost her son to these monsters! What kind of woman was she? Perhaps, all this time, he'd never truly known her.

Perhaps she'd always been a stranger.

And now she would have safe passage out of the country, and money as well, he was sure of it. How much had the lives of Guy and the others been worth? She'd probably never need to work again.

And then Rene remembered that, although Desiree had spent most of her life in France, she was still le Boche. She'd been born in the Sudetenland, after all, and obviously blood did indeed run thicker than water.

As he thought more about it, Rene's rage grew. All those years he had been a friend to Desiree; of helping her. He had loved her, and she'd never given him what she'd given so many others, friends and strangers alike. Somehow, he'd never been good enough for her. He'd always been jealous of all those others, even Mathieu, his good friend, because Mathieu had had her as well. Had it been him instead of Mathieu, Rene would never have let her go.

But now that jealousy was suddenly gone, along with the near-perfect vision of Desiree that he'd carried with him for so many years. She'd robbed Rene of that as well, left him empty, with nothing to have even the slightest hope for. And she'd soon be gone as well.

Rene went behind the counter in his restaurant, opened the drawer beneath the register. He carefully drew out his pistol and the extra box of bullets he kept with it. He checked the safety, loaded the gun and then tucked it into his belt.

"Nicholas!" he called. The boy was out back disposing of some empty cartons. He came quickly when he heard Rene's call.

"I need to borrow your bicycle," Rene told him.

***

There was nothing left to do now but wait. Desiree had long since settled everything as far as her business was concerned, and she'd carefully packed away the Francs she'd received in payment.

She had all her personal records; birth certificate, identity and ration card, although only the birth certificate would be needed, and perhaps the ration card until she crossed the border into Spain. When Desiree thought about it, she was surprised at how little she had after so many years spent in one place. But then she'd never acquired much in the way of belongings, and most of it would be left behind.

She had a few hours left before she could leave for Hans's townhouse, so Desiree decided to have a cup of coffee. She had debated about taking her coffee press, but decided it was the one luxury she would allow herself. It was still on her stove, near the water kettle. It would be one of the last things she'd pack, since she was still using it. She lit the stove and put the kettle on.

She thought of Hans as she waited for the water to boil. She had never felt for any man the way she felt for him. Not even Uwe. She knew that now.

He was so vulnerable, her Hans, even though he tried so hard to hide it. So much more vulnerable than she had ever imagined. Underneath a very cruel veneer there was an entirely different man, a boy, really; a lonely and torn child that matched the child that Desiree herself had been. There was something right about the two of them together. It wasn't that they formed a whole. How could they possibly do so when they were going to be parted?

No, it was more that they helped each other feel more whole. Desiree had never been the sentimental type, never believed that romantic love had any redemptive power. At one point she had thought that the love of parent for child had that power, but her own child's death had proved otherwise. No, love was not a redemptive force in and of itself. But maybe it could be an instrument of healing.

The kettle whistled. Desiree had already put coffee into the press. Now all she had to do was pour in the water and press the plunger down. A few minutes later she poured her cup of coffee, then added a little cream and sugar to it. She was about to sit down again when she heard the ring of a bicycle bell outside. She left her coffee on the table and moved to the door to see who was there.

"Rene. What is it?"

"Bonjour, Desiree."

Rene was unprepared for the rush of emotion he felt upon seeing her. He had loved her, after all. Those feelings couldn't just be turned off like a water tap. But he'd come there with a specific purpose, and regardless of how he felt about this woman, he would fulfill that purpose.

"Has something happened?" she asked.

"You know what's happened," he replied.

"What do you mean?"

"You've been part of it the entire time, haven't you?" He went on. "You and that SS Colonel."

Desiree went pale, which both steeled Rene's resolve and lit the furious rage inside him.

"You couldn't keep your legs shut, could you? Parting them for anyone and everyone; even a fucking Nazi. And not just any Nazi, but The Jew Killer himself."

"The Jew Killer?"

"That fucking Colonel of yours. Your lover. The one who hunts down the few Jews left and kills them."

Desiree caught her breath.

"Oh, you didn't know that about him? You'd never heard of the infamous Jew Killer?"

"I'd heard of him…"

"Yet you didn't put two and two together? You're a far more foolish woman than I'd thought. Or did lust simply blind you to the truth?"

"I didn't know," Desiree said quietly.

"And you expect me to believe that?"

Desiree's eyes snapped back to his. "Believe what you wish. Now get out of my house."

"Not without having you answer a few questions first."

Rene grabbed her roughly by the arm, pulled her to him. He was about to pull his gun when he caught her familiar scent. It filled him with despair. He pulled her closer to him, held her against his chest.

"Why did you do it?" he breathed, horrified to find himself close to tears. "Why did you betray Guy and the others?"

"I didn't," she said, "you know I didn't. I didn't even know they'd been arrested, don't you remember?"

"I remember," Rene said, "I do remember. But at the time I didn't know you were so well acquainted with the Colonel, the one responsible. You may not have known they'd been arrested, but who else would have given him the information to make those arrests?"

Desiree struggled to break free. "It wasn't me," she cried, "I swear it."

"Who else could it have been?"

"I don't know!"

"And what have we here?"

Hans stood in the doorway, smiling, his Walther drawn and trained on Rene. Both Rene and Desiree were dumbfounded. Hans entered the cottage, crossed over to the table, pulled out a chair and sat down. His eyes never left Rene, and the aim of his gun was steady.

"Don't let me interrupt you. Do go on."

Desiree gazed at him frantically. Hans's eyes locked on hers briefly and the message was clear: remain calm.

"Go on," he said, "continue your conversation. I'm very interested."

Rene looked him straight in the eye. "Did you expect no one would come for her? Your slut?" Just saying the last word filled Rene with pain.

Hans cocked his Walther. "If I were in your place," he began, slowly but calmly, "I'd be very, very careful of what I said."

"Do you believe I care what you think?"

"I would suggest you begin doing so. Just exactly what were you planning to do with her?"

"She's a collaborator." Rene felt his resolve weaken under Faber's sharp gaze.

"You think so? And what has she done?"

"You know what she's done. The people she's betrayed. You were part of it."

"Ah, I see," Hans said; his voice almost conversational. "Because she's shared my bed she must be a collaborator, is that it?"

"Obviously."

"Obviously? You know her so well, Charlont? You know exactly how she'd act in every circumstance?"

"Hans" Desiree pleaded.

"Shut up," he snapped at her, and once again his emerald eyes caught hers and held them for a moment, and something in those sharp eyes compelled her to keep quiet.

Hans turned to Rene, and a subtle change came over him. The face that had been relaxed and almost jovial seemed to harden from within. The shift in his expression was barely perceptible, and yet it was there. The jaw became firmer, the mouth still and set, the eyes steely. It was a chilling transformation and both Desiree and Rene shivered at the sight.

"You will remove your pistol from your pocket now," he told Rene, his voice level yet firm. "And place it on the table."

In one swift move Rene whipped out his pistol and aimed it at Hans. A shot rang out, and there was a cry of pain from Rene as his pistol clattered to the floor. In an instant Hans was out of his chair and had grabbed and pocketed it.

"Stay with him," he told Desiree, "don't worry." He kept his Walther trained on Rene, who had slumped to the floor, clutching his wrist. Blood was pouring from it. Desiree grabbed a kitchen towel and wrapped it around the wound to stem the flow. At the same time, Hans crossed quickly to the door to let in Hermann, who had his own Walther drawn and ready.

"Cuff him and take him to the town physician, then to the Geheime Statzpolizie" he told Hermann. "Then report to me at the townhouse."

"Jawohl, Standartenführer." Hermann crossed over to help Rene up from the floor. Desiree tried to help as well, but the look Rene gave her was so filled with hatred that she quickly backed away. She wished she could tell him the truth, but it was better to let Mathieu tell him after she'd left. Perhaps it would make a difference, perhaps not. Perhaps Rene would hate her for the rest of his life. It hurt terribly to think of it, but there was nothing she could do.

Hermann cuffed Rene and led him out of the cottage. "Take the bicycle, too," Hans called after him. After Rene had been seated in the car, Hans held his Walther on him while Hermann fetched and loaded the bicycle. When Hermann started the car and drove away, Hans turned to Desiree once more.

"You can't stay here any longer," he told her. "It isn't safe. You're coming home with me."

Together they bundled her few belongings and loaded them into her truck.

"Your business," Hans asked, "it's taken care of?"

"Yes."

"Do you have keys that need to be turned over to the new owners?"

"They have the keys already. To both the cottage and the storage shed. There's nothing else I need to do." She thought for a moment, then turned and dashed into the cottage.

"Desiree!!"

"I'll be right back; I've one more thing to get."

She quickly poured out her untouched coffee, rinsed the cup and saucer and the coffee press. She gazed at the cup and saucer in the dish drain as she toweled the parts of the coffee press dry. The set had belonged to her mother. It was one of the very few things she had left of her parents.

"Desiree! We've got to go!"

She took one last look at the cup and saucer before taking the now dry coffee press and exiting the cottage.

Hans opened the passenger side door of her truck and Desiree climbed in. He walked around the truck and climbed into the driver's seat, started the engine, and began driving.

Desiree took a last look at the cottage that had been her home longer than any other. She watched it recede in the distance as they drove further and further away, until at last it vanished from sight. Then she turned back to Hans.

Hans wrapped one arm around Desiree and pulled her close to him. She would never know just how close he came to killing Rene; how very much he wanted to tear limb from limb anyone who tried to harm her.

He held her tightly for the rest of the drive.

Chapter Nineteen

When they arrived at the townhouse, Hermann and Severine were already there, waiting for them. Severine gave Desiree a warm, welcoming hug while Hermann helped Hans unload Desiree's belongings. Desiree and Severine followed the two men as they carried the belongings upstairs to a small room close to Hans's bedroom.

"Your things will be safe here," Hans told Desiree. "Safe and accessible when you need them." He turned to Hermann. "How is Charlont?"

"The doctor said the bullet had only chipped a bone in his wrist, so he'll be fine, I imagine. He's in a cell at headquarters now."

"Oh, no," breathed Desiree. "Please, Hans…" Severine put her arm around Desiree to comfort her.

Hermann turned to Desiree, his blue eyes warm. "It's all right, Madame," he told her, "they're under strict orders to leave him alone as the Standartenführer's prisoner. No one will harm him."

Hans smiled. "Vielen dank, Hermann. I knew I could rely on you to do what needed to be done."

"Hans, what will happen to him?"

"I'll do my best," he told Desiree as the three started back downstairs. "After you're safely across the border in Spain he'll be charged with attempted murder of an SS officer. They won't shoot him; that was a pointless exercise I put a stop to, since it cost us valuable information about the Resistance throughout France. The policy now is to get as much information as possible from them, then send them to different camps."

He looked straight into Desiree's eyes. "I can't promise you anything about his future or his ultimate fate; to a certain extent that was sealed when he attempted to shoot me. He will go to a camp, where he'll be closely monitored to see if he makes contact with other Resistance members. The Resistance is like a tree with many branches. It's our goal to lop off each one while at the same time working on the roots."

"Is there anything at all you can do to help him?"

"I won't promise you anything. I couldn't, anyway. He was going to kill you…"

"I don't think he would have," Desiree told Hans. "I know he came to the cottage intending to do so, but he was already hesitating about it when you arrived…"

"As I said, I won't promise you anything." Hans held her gaze as he said it.

"The truck," he suddenly said, "do you need to deliver it somewhere?"

"Non. I was going to leave it at the cottage with the keys for the new owners."

"I'll have Hermann take it back, then." He handed the keys to Hermann.

"Put your motorbike in the back of the truck and return to your quarters afterward," he told him.

"Jawohl, Herr Standartenführer." There was a knock at the front door, and all three of them turned simultaneously toward it.

"That will be the guards, Herr Oberst," Hermann told Hans.

"Have them posted at every possible entryway. Madame Mendelsohn is at great risk, and we must keep her safe."

"Jawohl, Mein herr." Hermann opened the door and went outside to direct the guards to their positions.

"Dinner will be ready quite soon," Severine told Hans and Desiree. "Why don't you two have a drink in the parlor until then? You've barely had a moment to catch your breath."

"That's a splendid idea," Hans replied. "I'm sure we could both use one. What would you like?"

"I don't often drink it, but I'd like a whiskey now," Desiree told him as they both entered the parlor.

He gave her a wry smile. "Me, too," he said, as he poured them each a glass. He handed one to her and she took it without looking at him then sat down on one of the sofas. He eyed her curiously, then came and sat down beside her.

"What is it?"

"Rene said something about you," Desiree began.

"What did he say?"

"He said you were 'The Jew Killer'." She looked up into his eyes.

His face went through a subtle change; first it seemed to fall, but then it hardened.

"Yes," he said, "I've been called that."

"You find Jews and sometimes kill them on the spot."

"Yes," he said again. "I look for people. I'm a detective. I find people, enemies of the Reich…and some of them are Jews."

Desiree looked away and sat silent. Hans grasped her by the chin and turned her gently back to face him.

"It's what I do. It's my job," he told her. "I won't pretend it's not part of who I am, because it is."

"But to hunt people down; to kill them just because they're Jews."

"I could care less about that. I don't distinguish between the people I find. I simply do my job to the best of my ability."

Desiree looked at him in despair.

"This is who I am," Hans went on. "Am I a monster because of it? No. I'm just a man. Nothing more, nothing less." He got up from the sofa and began to pace around it.

"No doubt it would be better if I was a monster. If I was some demon from another world, evil personified. That would be easier to understand, wouldn't it? For me to be a hideous, inhuman creature instead of your lover."

"Yes," Desiree whispered.

"I'm not. I'm a man who loves you. Do you hate me now?"

"I can't hate you," she breathed. "Even if I wanted to, I couldn't."

Hans stopped next to her and laid a hand against her cheek, and instinctively Desiree leaned into that hand. With his other hand he began to stroke her hair.

There was a knock on the parlor door. "I have your dinner, M. Colonel."

Hans crossed over to the double doors and opened them to let in Severine with the tray. It was a simple meal. Hans liked all his meals simple. There were slices of prime rib, sautéed green beans with sliced mushrooms, roasted potatoes with rosemary and a fine Cabernet.

It could have been straw for all Desiree was concerned. She ate mechanically, refusing to look at Hans as she did so.

"Look at me," he said finally.

She did, and she saw a man very dear to her. A man who had hunted people down; had killed them, but had also touched her, made love to her; a man who in fact loved her, body and soul.

Hadn't she always known this about him? She'd even told him once that she didn't care if he'd killed people. What made things different now? That he had a nickname associated with terror and death? That terror and death were also an intrinsic part of his nature?

She had actually seen Uwe kill, after all, and she had loved him and still did. But Uwe had changed. He wasn't the same man by the time he'd freed her. He hadn't summarily killed anyone again in the camp.

Desiree looked into Hans's eyes again. Had he changed? He could have killed Rene, she was sure of it; yet he hadn't. Was it possible he had truly changed the way Uwe had?

But would it matter if he hadn't? What if he was still the same man? After she left she'd never know whether he killed again. In the insane world they both occupied, would it matter if the man she loved was capable of killing? Was it at all possible to reconcile these two indisputable facts? And again; did it matter? Did any of it matter?

Hans's eyes were a brilliant emerald green again, and there was that sharpness, that radiance in them to which she had responded so strongly from the very first night they'd met. But now there was something else in them as well; a longing, a hunger that flashed brightly but then vanished quickly, as though a steel door suddenly came crashing down, cutting off the light that had been there.

"I am who I am, Desiree," Hans told her quietly. "I'm a killer. I can't change the past. I can't change what I've done or who I've been."

"But you can change your present," Desiree replied. "You already have. You're not the same man you were before you met me, are you?"

Hans thought about that for a moment.

"No," he finally replied, "not all of me. But there are some aspects of my character that nothing and no one can change, not even you."

"I know that," Desiree said. "I've always known that."

"Then what's changed since you learned I was 'The Jew Killer'? How am I different now?"

There was another knock at the door, and Severine came in to clear up.

"It was delicious, as always," Hans told her, "thank you."

"Yes, thank you, Severine," added Desiree.

Severine smiled in return. "I'll be back momentarily with coffee and dessert. I've made a berry tart today."

"That sounds wonderful. Bring it right in," said Hans.

They were both quiet until Severine returned with the coffee and the tart.

"I'll serve us," Desiree told her. "Thank you so much, it looks wonderful."

"It does indeed," echoed Hans.

"Merci beaucoup, M. Colonel et Mme Mendelsohn."

"Oh please, Severine, do call me Desiree, just the way you did when we worked together."

Severine gave her a fond smile, then wrapped an arm around the seated Desiree's shoulders and gave her a quick squeeze. Then she stood tall and looked Hans right in the eye.

"M. Colonel," she began, "pardonnez-mois, but I must speak my mind."

Hans cocked an eyebrow, and Desiree looked up at Severine in surprise.

"Mme Desiree is a good woman," she went on, "whatever she does… or has done…please protect her. Please keep her safe."

Hans returned Severine's steady gaze, and Desiree watched that steel door rise and the warmth return to those bright, emerald eyes.

"You needn't worry, Severine," he told her. "I won't let any harm come to her."

Severine gave Desiree another affectionate squeeze. "Merci beaucoup, M. Colonel."

After Severine had left, Hans turned to Desiree and watched her cut and serve the tart and pour their coffee.

"It's different now, isn't it," he said, his voice softer. "Different than it was ten minutes ago, and different still from three hours ago."

Desiree looked up at him.

"I'm different. You're different," he continued. "And yet we're also the same. I'm still a ruthless and angry man. I'm still 'The Jew Killer'. And you? You're still brave and honorable and terrified and so very, very generous although you'd never admit it.

"Two hours from now we'll each, again, be different people, but at the core we'll each remain the same."

"Yes," Desiree replied. "Different, and yet the same."

***

They went upstairs together not long after they'd finished their dessert and Severine had cleared everything away. They undressed and got into bed like any long-married couple, with no more than a quick kiss. They both felt uneasy, as though by sharing a fundamental, unchangeable secret they'd each become more vulnerable to the other. And, despite everything they'd said, it was as though a wound remained between them, one that stubbornly refused to heal.

Desiree lay on her side, facing away from Hans, and he lay on his back, staring up at the ceiling.

They were quiet for a long time, listening only to each other's breathing.

Then Desiree heard Hans turn and felt him reach out for her, placing a hand on her hip and gently stroking it.

It was an appeal of sorts, an expression of need and desire and affection so simple and unadorned that Desiree felt a sharp pang in her belly in response. She turned to Hans and was immediately gathered up in his arms and passionately, passionately kissed.

There was a greater urgency in the way they now kissed and touched; far greater than they'd ever before experienced together, a hunger so desperate that appeasing it seemed almost impossible. And yet they tried so hard to do so. They groped, grasped, clawed, licked, nibbled, gnawed and bit at each other, and when they were at last joined it was fiery and intense and they moaned from the pleasure of it.

They sat up, facing each other, and rocked together violently, clinging desperately to each other, their mouths and their hips joined.

Hans suddenly pushed Desiree back against the bed, pulled out and quickly buried his face between her legs, noisily licking, sucking and nipping at her wet flesh until she cried out and came, and then he flipped her onto her belly, lifted her hips and plunged inside her once more.

When he was completely, deeply inside her, Hans held still and let loose a low, deep, primal moan that seemed to come from the depths of his soul, which Desiree echoed with a moan just as primal and deep. Hans held her hips to him and began moving slowly, drawing the full length of his cock in and out. Rather than increase in speed, he drew out each thrust even longer, so they could both enjoy the slow, slick, almost torturous friction of their joined flesh.

Desiree felt as though she might go mad from that exceedingly slow rhythm, the long draw of that stiff cock inward and outward, and she whimpered and struggled to increase the almost dream-like sexual tempo. It was too much; too much sensation, too much feeling. She could hardly bear it.

And then Hans lowered down and pressed against her. She felt the soft hairs on his chest caress her back and his hot breath in her ear.

"Only I can give you this," he whispered. "No one else. Ever." He licked her ear, then bit it, and Desiree shuddered with pleasure. "Ja, meine liebe, feel how deeply I can touch you…"

"Please, Hans," she whimpered. "Please…I need…"

"What do you need?" He kept his thrusts steady.

"I need to feel you…"

"I'm right here, Liebchen, deep inside you. Can you feel me?"

"Oui…oh, more, please…"

"Bitte?"

"Bitte," she moaned.

"Like this?" He increased both the depth and speed of his thrusts, and drank in each sweet sound of pleasure that issued from her mouth.

"Ja," he breathed, "your sounds; give me your moans, your sighs, I need them…"

He grasped her hips, moving harder and deeper, listening closely as her moans grew longer and deeper.

"Ja…mehr…mehr"

And then the two of them began to moan together, Hans pausing only to kiss her cheeks and gnaw at her throat, to taste and touch her as much as possible.

It seemed to grow slowly, the very acuteness of their shared pleasure; wave after wave after wave of a tremendous build, build, build, as though a thousand new worlds were being born until Desiree arched back against Hans, clutching him, grasping him tightly, rhythmically inside her as the ache grew and grew and grew until it flew apart in a thousand pieces, and she was coming so powerfully she couldn't catch her breath, and barely felt his teeth sink into her shoulder as he followed her.

Hans wrapped himself around Desiree afterwards and held her close, kissing her tenderly, and she thought suddenly of Uwe and the very first time he had held her like this. A connection was made then; it snapped firmly in place, and a treasured circle closed to keep it safe within her.

***

"You're so soft," Hans whispered. He lay behind Desiree once more, one arm reaching around to stroke her belly. "I love to touch you…"

Desiree laid her hand over his.

"I'll miss this," Hans said. "I'll miss it terribly."

"I will, too."

Hans buried his face in her shoulder and kissed tenderly the spot he'd bitten earlier.

"Ich liebe dich," he whispered.

"Je t'aime," she answered, bringing his hand to her mouth and kissing it.

***

Next morning Hans finished his coffee, put the cup back into the saucer and rose, grabbing his cap and gloves. "What will you do today?"

"I'll help Severine around the house," Desiree replied, "make myself useful."

Hans grinned at that. "She's a good woman," he told Desiree, "and she likes you. It's a rather nice way to spend your last…" he stopped.

"…my last days here. I agree."

She saw the flicker of pain pass through his eyes, then watched them grow strong and reassuring again.

"Come," Hans said, putting on his cap and then his gloves. "Kiss me goodbye. We'll pretend to be husband and wife."

Desiree's smile matched his as she rose and walked over to him.

Chapter Twenty

"Like this," Hans whispered, as he lifted Desiree's left knee over his shoulder. They had already made love twice that night, but were still so hungry for each other.

Desiree moved as if to lift her right leg as well, but "No," he whispered, "this one stays down."

"Please put it in," she pleaded, "please…"

"Ja, meine liebe," he breathed as he slowly slid inside her. Gott, why did each time he entered her give him such incredible pleasure? He moved slowly inside her, savoring each thrust as she moved to meet him, and they quickly found that incredible rhythm they'd created together.

Their eyes remained open and they gazed steadily at each other, unable to close them or turn away. Desiree was riveted by his face, by how open and elementally human it looked, so different from the man in uniform; as though his soul were bared when he was lost in ecstasy. It made her ache to see it and she clung tightly to him, luxuriating in each press of their flesh together.

His eyes were shining, two beautiful deep emerald orbs in his handsome face, his lips were parted and he was breathing very deeply; his skin was warm and damp with sweat, and his musky, male scent filled her nostrils. Desiree drank it all in: she wanted to commit all of it to memory. She never wanted to forget this experience, this man, this sharing of their love.

Hans was doing the same, committing all of what they were sharing to his memory, to be brought out when the need to remember grew too great; if he could bear to remember at all. He feared he might not be able to do so, that he might instead bury all this beauty deep inside him to avoid the pain that would surely come with remembering.

The need for the oblivion of pleasure grew stronger at the very thought of this, and Hans clung to Desiree and kissed her fiercely as it approached. He could feel that she was close, too, and their rhythms matched until together they were bathed in a shower of bliss.

Afterwards, Desiree reached up to touch Hans's face. As the time of their parting drew near there were frequently tears in his eyes; tears she knew he'd never let loose. His anguish tore at her, and she pulled him down and held him close to kiss the corners of his eyes, drawing the tears out and kissing them off his cheeks.

***

During those last days Desiree worked with Severine around the house, making herself as useful as she could. At first they didn't talk of what was to come, but then one evening they were preparing dinner together when Desiree suddenly spoke.

"Severine," she began, "I must ask something of you."

"What do you need? I'll be happy to do it for you."

Desiree turned to her and smiled. Severine had become a good friend to her. To her and Hans both.

"It's not for me," she went on, "it's the Colonel. Look after him for me, will you? Don't…let him get all hardened again."

"I'm not sure there's much I can do to prevent that," Severine told her. "He is the man he is. There's that soft core inside him," she turned to Desiree, "that core which makes it possible for him to love you, but he will do what he has to do to protect that core and himself."

"I know," Desiree replied, "and that's what worries me. Inside he's somehow very fragile, but outside…"

"The outside has to protect the inside, because the one thing that frightens him, perhaps the only thing that frightens him, is weakness. He can't bear the thought of being weak."

"He doesn't realize that he needs to let himself experience weakness to become truly strong," Desiree said.

"And I don't believe he ever will," replied Severine.

The two women gazed at each other in despair. There was so little they could do to help the man they both cared for so deeply.

***

Hans arranged to have that last day off so he could spend some time with Desiree. The morning she was to leave he and Hermann would provide her with escort to the first checkpoint in her journey.

She'd asked after Charlont a couple of times. He told her that the man would remain in custody for questioning, and that was all he told her. He couldn't bring himself to tell Desiree that he hadn't been able to delay the Gestapo from launching their interrogation of Charlont. As Hans had suspected, he was far too important a link in the Resistance chain.

There was nothing he could have done to prevent it, so there was no sense in Desiree knowing about it. Hans had no regrets for not telling her; he didn't want anything to ruin these last days they had together. In the end it wouldn't make any difference whether or not she knew. The outcome would be the same. The Gestapo would get the information they needed, and Charlont would be executed. It was only what the man deserved, after all.

All that mattered to Hans now was Desiree. In the evenings he would go home, they would have dinner and talk and then go to bed to make love, talk some more, and then make love again until they finally fell asleep from exhaustion. Sleep mattered little. Hans couldn't get enough of Desiree - he knew he never would - but damned if he wouldn't at least try to fill their final days together with a lifetime's worth of the love he felt for her.

Time was passing so quickly, but he didn't want to think about that.

***

Desiree lay next to Hans and drew her lips all over his body—not kissing, not nibbling, just letting her lips brush lightly against his skin so she could truly feel its warmth and texture. Her touch was so light that Hans shivered with pleasure. It was a teasing yet tender touch, so loving that he was soon trembling all over.

His skin felt alive; every aspect of him felt alive, body and soul. All of those years of never being touched and of wanting it so desperately hadn't been in vain. He was being touched now in ways he never had been; ways he never even knew existed.

Desiree let her long, soft hair brush along his body, dusting it, the whirls and swirls of those dark tresses caressing every inch of his flesh. And then the very tips of her fingers touched him so lightly, so gently, drawing slow trails along his chest, his abdomen and each of his limbs, from his shoulders to the tip of each finger, from his hips down to his toes.

All of it only made him hungrier for her, so that when her mouth at last engulfed him he gasped, so aroused and excited that release came very quickly.

Afterwards he lay back, shuddering and gasping for breath, and waited for her to crawl back up his body so that he could pull her into a crushingly passionate embrace.

Then it was his turn. Hans used his lips and tongue to draw soft lines and delicate circles along Desiree's body. She was so incredibly soft and sweet; he felt as though he could never get enough of the taste of her skin. When at last he moved his mouth between her legs, he moaned with delight at the first touch of his tongue to that silky wet flesh. He exulted in the pleasure he gave her and how she trembled and gripped him with her thighs when she found her own release.

As urgent as their passion was during these last days, it seemed somehow appropriate to move slowly in pleasing each other, to savor every taste and touch. It was as if by prolonging their pleasure they could somehow beat back time, hold back the inevitable and delay their ultimate parting.

But there was always that other purpose to their slow rhythm for Hans. It was that desperate need to memorize every aspect of this woman who meant more to him than any other woman he had ever known. Remember this, he told himself. Remember all of it, all of her, this woman you love so much. Memorize her and keep her safely inside you, forever.

***

Desiree lay against Hans, lightly stroking the soft dusting of hair on his chest. Hans closed his eyes and let himself enjoy her gentle touch, then brought a hand up to stroke her hair.

"It's good that you speak English, as I do," he told her. "I've always wanted to go to America. New York, Chicago, Hollywood; you can leave the past behind, start afresh, lead a new life."

"A new country always offers the chance to build a new life," Desiree replied.

"Yes, but America is different," Hans said. "Everything new and modern is in America. It's a country built solely on the premise of creating a new way of life, one very different than in Europe. That's why it's the 'new' world."

"It's so enormous, this new world. I wonder what I'll do there."

"You'll cook, of course. The money you'll have will be enough to get you settled, but it's where you settle that will make a difference. You'll arrive in New York, but I wouldn't stay there."

"It's too big for me. Too crowded."

"I agree. It would be too easy for you to get lost there, even with your culinary talents. It's better to start off somewhere smaller."

"Where shall I go, then?"

Hans turned to her, a thoughtful look on his face as he considered the possibilities. Then he smiled.

"The North-eastern coast is called New England," he began. "I've heard it's a wonderful place. The people who live there respect privacy or so I'm told. They're stolid and strong and keep to themselves. But it's also an area with many quaint and charming towns that attract visitors on holiday, and all these towns have restaurants. That makes it the perfect place for you to start your career and build a new life."

"Is it a state or a region?"

"A region. It includes all the states from Pennsylvania upwards, including New Hampshire, Massachusetts, Maine," Hans broke off.

"What is it?"

"Maine," he replied. "There's a small town there. Yes, I know where you should go. Gardiner, off the coast of Maine."

***

The last night.

Their last night together.

They clung to each other, never wanting to let go.

Their kisses were ardent and loving, their caresses tender and passionate.

They made love for the very last time.

***

They arose early that final morning, dressed quickly and went downstairs, to be greeted by Severine with a hearty breakfast. They were all rather grim while Severine poured the coffee. Desiree looked up to thank her and saw the tears in the older woman's soft, grey eyes. She got up immediately and wrapped her arms around Severine, drawing her into a strong hug.

When they drew apart, Severine sighed as she wiped away her tears. "It's foolish, I know," she said. "You're going where you'll be safe. I shouldn't cry for that."

"I'll miss you, too, Severine," Desiree told her, giving her another quick hug and a kiss on her cheek. "I'll miss you more than you can ever know."

"Oh, don't be foolish," Severine replied. "Don't waste time thinking about me or the past. Focus on the future. Just don't forget him," she said nodding towards Hans.

Desiree looked at Hans, and their eyes locked. "I never could," she told Severine.

***

Later that morning, as Hermann drove them out of town, Hans kept his arm tight around Desiree and held her close. Desiree thought of Severine, of Mathieu and his family, and of Rene, who was still imprisoned. All were people who had been important to her, and she was leaving them behind now, possibly, no, probably, forever. She was leaving Hans, too, but she couldn't bring herself to even consider the prospect of never seeing him again. It hurt too much to do so.

Hans tried very hard not to think of what was now finally happening. He focused on the details of the journey as much as possible, but he couldn't help feeling as though time itself was ticking off the minutes of their last hours together. He would be with Desiree until the first checkpoint, where they would drop her off for the next leg of her journey.

When, at last, they had arrived at the checkpoint, Hans drew Desiree close and hugged and kissed her deeply for several long, precious minutes.

"You'll be safe from here on," he told her when he at last drew back. "You'll have nothing to worry about. All the arrangements have been made and your papers are in order. You should have a very smooth journey."

Desiree could see how hard he was struggling to maintain that calm and collected façade. She reached up to touch his face and he leaned into that touch.

"I love you," she told him.

Hans barely held his composure as he reached out to caress her cheek. Somehow he managed to smile at her. "And I love you," he replied. "Be safe. And don't forget me."

"I never could," she said once again, before they kissed for the last time. When they finally drew apart he paused to whisper in her ear, "Ich liebe dich."

As he watched Desiree being driven away to her next checkpoint, Hans could feel the chill move into his heart once more, and he welcomed it. Without it, he was sure he could never survive what was happening to him now. That chill would keep him alive, keep him functioning. It would bury all he felt for Desiree; freeze those feelings and keep them safe, forever, right alongside the love he'd buried for Jürgen.

One Month Later

Hans had very quickly discovered that life went on, just as it always had. The first few nights without Desiree had been almost unbearable, and he'd compensated for that by drinking more wine with dinner and brandy after. It helped to dull the pain, but he knew that alcohol was not only a temporary panacea but also an unhealthy one, so he began going to the officers' gymnasium on a regular basis. He made use of the weights there to strengthen his body, which he'd always felt was too thin. He also began running again; up to five miles a day. He'd heard that Rommel did so to both stay in shape and keep his senses sharp, and Hans found that it worked.

And then there was Strasser. It hadn't been difficult at all to seduce him. After their first dinner together he was easily lured back to Hans's townhouse for a nightcap, and quickly ended up in Hans's bed. They met frequently after that. The sex was always rough, always violent. Hans would beat him, strangle him, fuck him brutally; but the boy kept coming back for more.

Sex had always been good for Hans, and it was remarkably good with Strasser, who was an exceptionally pliable, willing and responsive partner. He was beautiful, too, with skin as pale as porcelain and soft like a woman's, yet firm like a man's; a long, slender cock that sprung to life at Hans's very touch and that incredible red mouth with its luscious lips that looked so pretty wrapped around his cock and always trembled with a quavering moan when he came.

He thoroughly enjoyed touching and tasting the boy, licking the sweat from his limbs, biting his tender nipples and his soft throat, slapping and beating and whipping him. And fucking him was absolutely delightful. Strasser had been a slut for cock since he was twelve, and Hans found it deeply satisfying to penetrate him and release his seed inside him, marking the young man forever as his property. Indeed, Strasser was very quickly becoming Hans's favorite plaything, and Hans enjoyed finding new ways to take him well beyond his boundaries.

But none of it was ever enough to satisfy him, and it never would be enough. Hans knew that now. He couldn't, no; wouldn't, think of what was missing. It hurt too much. It was far easier to shut down that part of him as much as possible, to unleash what he could of his rage and despair with Strasser or with one of the whores at Mme. Henriette's, where he had been welcomed back with open arms.

There were even times when he sought out the rent boy in that dark alley, when he needed those deep brown eyes, that soft, dark hair that so reminded him of Desiree. When he was deep inside him, Hans would wrap his arms around the lad, hold him close, kiss the soft curls at the back of his neck and remember; and yet not remember. Those were the times when he came with an intensity so fierce it left him breathless.

But there was never that complete sense of letting go that he had experienced with Desiree; something Hans hadn't experienced with anyone else except Jürgen. Even when his body was awash in the afterglow of orgasm and his limbs heavy with satiation, his mind and his soul remained hollow and unsatisfied.

Desiree and Jürgen; they were the first two people he thought of when he awoke every morning, and the last two people he thought of when he at last lay his weary head down to sleep at night. He knew Desiree had boarded the ship safely, and was on her way to America. And he was sure she would settle in Gardiner, Maine, as he'd recommended. It was the perfect place for her, and she would surely find good work in a restaurant there.

Jürgen was another matter. They'd had one last exchange of letters before Jürgen's unit was directed to join the 6th Army at Stalingrad, now embroiled in a fierce battle that would be made far more difficult by the approaching winter. Despite Goebbels' spluttering over the radio about an inevitable victory, Hans and others in the SD were beginning to doubt that Germany would prevail. After all, not even Napoleon had been able to withstand the ferocity of a Russian winter. Hans knew it was only a matter of time. He also knew that Jürgen, as an officer, would suffer deeply at the hands of the Red Army. Hans had frequent nightmares about this, and often woke up in a cold sweat.

But he also dreamed of Desiree, dreams so real that he could feel her soft skin and smell her sweet scent. Hans would wake up achingly hard then, and bring himself off while biting back phantom tears; tears he might have let take shape and perhaps spill over had he let himself feel. But he didn't want to feel anything. Yet, at the same time, he knew that he could never completely bury his feelings. The void in his life only made him feel more, and as much as he tried to fill it with Strasser, with whores, with the rent boy, with exercise, with drink, he never could.

Only one thing truly kept Hans going, made all that ill-buried feeling tolerable enough to keep him focused on his job, to keep him moving forward through the war.

Gardiner, Maine.

Whatever it took to do so, after the war Hans would travel there to find Desiree. He was determined to do absolutely anything to make that happen. Mountains would be moved. Countries would crumble. Perhaps the very Reich itself would fall.

***

They would be in New York harbor soon. Desiree leaned against the ship's railing, waiting for the famous Statue of Liberty to appear on the horizon.

It had been a long and difficult trip, and soon it would be over. There had been a couple of scares; first at the Spanish border, then at the Portuguese one, but she and her guide had gotten through each time.

Yet it wasn't until the Port of Lisbon could no longer be seen from the deck of the ship that Desiree at last felt safe.

Not that there weren't risks during that transatlantic journey. There were German U-boats in the waters, but somehow they managed to cross without incident.

Desiree had stayed in her cabin at first, not wanting to mingle with the other passengers. She was in mourning, after all, for a life left behind and the people who had been part of it, both the living and the dead.

She came out for meals and when she needed to visit the ship's library to pick up another book. She had decided to read only books in English to strengthen her knowledge of the language. Then, once a day, she took a walk around the deck. It was on one of these walks when Daniel first spoke to her. She'd seen him in the ship's dining room at every meal, sitting alone, just as she did, and in the library occasionally. He was younger than she by a good fifteen years or more, but his dark eyes seemed to bear a century's worth of sadness.

After that first meeting he sat with her at all the meals, accompanied her to the library and on her walks; which became more frequent as they practiced their English with each other. It was during these walks when Desiree learned what was behind Daniel's haunted eyes and shell-shocked demeanor. He was a Polish Jew who had somehow made his way out of the Warsaw ghetto. His parents had died there, while two brothers and a sister had been deported to the East. There were rumors about their destination, but Daniel preferred not to believe them; he still held hope that the rumors were untrue, or that perhaps his siblings had escaped. Anything but what his mind refused to acknowledge.

It was perhaps inevitable that she and Daniel would make love. They had each lost and left behind so much. But Desiree found that she'd never before felt so removed from her partner during sex. It was as though she was observing the two of them together from a distance. He gave her pleasure, but she couldn't ignore the fact that he smelled, tasted and felt very different from her Hans, and it was when she was in Daniel's arms that Desiree realized how horribly she missed the man she loved. She struggled not to let it show. She didn't want to hurt Daniel; he'd been hurt enough. But somehow he knew, perhaps because he, too, was holding back his feelings.

It happened twice, and each time, afterwards, they had both felt quite awkward with each other. They decided not to repeat the experience, but out of habit they continued to dine and walk together, and were generally considered a couple by passengers and crew alike.

Now, as she gazed over the railing, Desiree's eyes suddenly caught a shape in the distant horizon; could it be? Yes. She could see it now, faintly, towering over the dark shape of what must be the famed skyscrapers of Manhattan - the Statue of Liberty. They were nearing New York harbor at last.

Daniel approached and stood beside her. The two of them gazed together at the horizon, watching the Statue of Liberty grow larger as the ship moved closer to the harbor. At last Daniel turned to her.

"What will you do when you disembark?" He asked. "Where will you go?"

Desiree didn't answer.

"My cousins; I'm sure we can take you in."

"That's not necessary," she told him. "Once I've gone through Ellis Island I'll only be in New York overnight before I leave for Maine."

Daniel took her hand and pressed a folded piece of paper into it.

"My address and telephone," he said. "Don't forget to contact me once you've gotten settled."

She smiled and took the paper, but said nothing.

They stood side by side in silence as the ship approached the harbor. When they had entered it, Daniel turned towards Desiree once more. It was then she noticed that his dark eyes were no longer sad when he looked at her. She could read hope in them now.

He smiled at her, and she could also clearly see that he was no longer the haunted man he had been when they'd first met. "We're each disembarking at different points," he told her, "so I've got to get back to my cabin now, to gather my luggage and get ready to meet my cousins."

Daniel turned as though to leave, but hesitated; suddenly he pulled her into his arms and kissed her, quickly but with great enthusiasm. When he let her go he held onto her shoulders for a moment.

"You'll be all right, then, on your own? We shan't see each other once I disembark."

She smiled back at him, patted his hand on her shoulder.

"I'll be fine," she replied. "Don't worry about me."

"I'll see you, then," he said. "Contact me as soon as you've gotten settled. You have my telephone number and address now."

Desiree lifted her hand with the paper to confirm this. Daniel grinned, then turned to hurry to his cabin.

He'd been gone for ten minutes when she at last examined the folded piece of paper he'd given her. She held it for a while, but didn't unfold it.

Finally, her face grim, Desiree tore the folded paper into quarters and dropped them over the deck, into the waters of New York harbor. She watched them float away on the dancing waves.

Once again she was breaking that vow she'd made to herself what seemed like years ago now; the vow that she would never again hurt anyone. But it really couldn't be helped this time. How could she, a woman who had loved two Nazis, ever become involved with a Jew who had lost his entire family to them? Daniel would never understand it in a thousand years, and it would only hurt him deeply.

She could never tell him, but at the same time she would not be able to avoid doing so. No, it was absolutely impossible. For there was another, much more important reason she could never pursue a relationship with Daniel.

Desiree hadn't expected it to happen. She'd thought she was too old. It wasn't until she was halfway across the Atlantic that she knew.

She rested a gentle hand on her belly and gazed down at her most precious cargo –
Hans's child.

Epilogue

Two long years passed, and finally, the war came to an end. Hans had been prepared for it. Never an ardent Nazi, he was an opportunist first, and when he was captured it was easy to turn evidence against his superiors. He did so for more than one reason. To save his own hide, of course, but he was bound and determined to do much more. He made a deal for himself. Passage to America. There was, after all, a reason he had been so specific in telling Desiree where to go in that vast, sprawling new world.

Gardiner, Maine.

It wasn't long before he was in a US military plane, on his way to America.

He didn't care what it took. He would find Desiree. He would have her again, and for the rest of his life.

And if that wasn't love, Hans had no idea what else it could possibly be.

The End

www.blackvelvetseductions.com

About the author

Born in Berkeley, California, Deborah Kelsey was raised in Orinda, California; Columbo, Ceylon (now Sri Lanka); and New Delhi, India. During her childhood she traveled throughout Asia and Europe with her family, as well as throughout the United States. She looks forward to traveling again in the not-so-distant future. A professional writer for over 30 years, she is also the author of Robert Siodmak: A Biography, with Analyses of his Films Noirs and a Complete Filmography of his Works. She currently makes her home in Southern California.